# *Willow Dawn*

A novella by Danielle Aubrey

This book is a work of fiction and written for entertainment purposes only. All places, people, and stories are figments of the author's imagination and not factual events or individuals.

Quotes and content from this book are authorized for entertainment only and any use must cite the author for credit.

Unauthorized reproduction of this book by any individual or entity is prohibited.

© 2022 Danielle McCallister All rights reserved
Cover design: Casey Arbogast
Cover photo: Payton Wilson-Hooks

"When all the dust is settled and all the crowds are gone, the things that matter are faith, family, and friends."
- Barbara Bush

It was the last week of Jordan's tour and Willow's mom Ror was busy working the merch table. Her dad Max was waiting backstage to complete the post soundcheck routine so J could avoid being around too many fans which always made him panicky.

As she did during every other show, Willow watched the Valentine's Day performance from backstage. Just before it wrapped up, she ran out the side door and caught the big reveal from the back of the crowd like she was just any other spectator. She never tired of seeing J stand up and turn around to face the crowd for the first time all night. His approach was weird, and it drew crowds of people she didn't understand, adults with money that used big words and always seemed just a little too big for their britches. That's how her mom had described them, and it seemed to fit; she later found that this pretentious crowd was interested in the novelty of J's gift and understood his rare talent and uncommon style. Performing with his back to them only seemed to feed their curiosity of his showmanship and when he turned around, the crowd would always gasp at seeing his glorious red beard and such beautifully strange movement. It was enough to cause an explosion of applause and Willow got drunk off the energy and wept with pride every time.

His bow and exit were a fluid singular movement and as soon as he ran off stage, Willow loved to run outside and let the rush of air sting her wet cheeks. It had become tradition and that night was no different.

She waved at her mom as she headed outside. They were in Atlanta and the air bit at her as she stepped out. Willow looked up at the starry sky and wondered how even with the pollution from all the lights, it was so bright and beautiful. She laughed as the adrenaline began to drain from her buzzing body and her ears still rang with the language of J's art. Wondering if she was alone in her excitement, she looked around to see who else was milling about.

There were three couples making their way into the night. She marveled at what love looked like on each one of them. One pair looked absolutely smitten with one another as they held hands and smiled shyly when their partner said something flattering. The other four middle aged lovers seemed stuffier but comfortable. She wondered what love felt like and Willow's heart raced as she thought about the boy she had been pining for back home in Avery for two years.

As her favorite of the three pairs passed by, she hugged her arms around herself for warmth but couldn't stop from blurting out to them. "You guys are so cute together!"

The taller of the two smiled at her beau and winked before saying, "Thanks, girl. Find one that loves all of you, not just the smooth edges. Trust me, he's got his hands full." She smiled at him, and he put his arm around her waist and pulled her in close. "Well, that's for sure," he said and smirked. As he kissed his girlfriend's head, he looked at Willow with what seemed like concern, "For real though, you must not be from here. You really should get inside soon; a girl shouldn't be running around this city alone, especially at night."

    She returned the smile but accepted his warning, turning on her heel to head back in. Her mind was still clear through the next several minutes and as she walked toward the door, Willow caught the eye of a handsome stranger she had somehow missed in her burst out into the cold. He was a kid like her, but a little older; he could have been sixteen or maybe seventeen? He was smoking, and his warm wintry clothes said that unlike her, he *was* from around there. She suddenly forgot what cold was or that she had ever seen (let alone crushed on) any other guy.

    Like she had done it millions of times, Willow plucked the cigarette out of his hand and took a drag, then another before handing it back. Brazenness had never been something she had lacked, but it helped that she had tried cigarettes a couple of times and remembered how to breathe the smoke in-kind of.

The smoke was heavy in her chest, and it burned with a delicious flavor she didn't recognize. Then the coughing started, and she fought to catch her breath as her lungs caught fire.

The handsome stranger smirked, and Willow's brain began to fuzz around the edges. He took her hand and kissed it mysteriously without offering a name. She blushed in return (although he didn't notice with the flush she had developed in the chilly air). He was drinking from a coffee mug and offered a swig. *Wow. Really going all in on this one, aren't you?* Her conscience judged her for the stupid girl she was being, and Willow swiftly ignored it. As what she had come to presume was weed began to really set in, she realized the danger and strangeness of the situation and momentarily allowed that inner gripe to examine the scene. The crowd hadn't yet let out and for just a few moments longer the night belonged to her and the criminally hot guy.

Obviously, the mug was full of booze that only added to the hell in her chest. She took another two hits of his joint in hopes of extinguishing the pain, only to light it up all over again. As she was gagging down several more swigs of alcohol, two other guys walked up that looked to be about the same age as the kid she was crushing on.

Willow couldn't focus much because she was trying to catch her breath, but she heard them say they were going to catch up with their dads since the concert was over but would see him at the party later. She could have sworn she heard them call him Rick or something. It seemed like an old and boring name for a kid, but she didn't have time to ponder as she continued to fight the flames inside her. By the time she righted herself, his cronies were long gone.

    Her new acquaintance said something about he and his friends coming to the show because his dad thought it would make him more appealing in the upcoming election. However, the Rick kid claimed he just wanted to go home and get ready for the kegger that someone was having. It was all starting to blur together, but she remembered that comment because she wondered what a kegger was and why he wanted to be there so badly. Willow gathered that he was going to drive them all home after the party since he was the only one with a car. He asked if she wanted to see his ride and, she said she did. Looking back, she was always so ashamed that she never saw what was coming next.

    They rounded the block and Willow had a panicked realization that super-hot or not, she genuinely didn't know the first thing about the guy she was alone with. Her heart jumped with fear, but she convinced herself that she was stupid for being afraid; she wasn't in danger.

Just as a slick red sports car came into view, her phone rang. It was her dad.

Her mind was muddled, and she had to have sounded like she was in slow motion (because that's exactly how it felt). Somehow, she managed to conjure up a quick lie about some girls she'd met and was exchanging numbers with outside. Her Dad was with J on the bus and asked her to meet him there in ten minutes. She looked at her new companion and smiled. "Sure Dad, ten minutes. I'll be there."

They approached the guy's impressive ride, and he opened the door and slid the passenger seat forward. Willow was stoned and drunk but not stupid. She shook her head and told him she wasn't getting back there unless he went first. He smiled and crawled in with her close behind. Without further conversation he was peeling off his coat and wrapping it around her frigid arms that wore only a camo sweatshirt. He kissed her with an intensity that she couldn't deny and everything he did felt like it was meant for her. She was new to all of it, and he was her first everything. She was so awkward, but he didn't seem to care.

She would never fully remember the order of their actions, only that at some point he offered more booze and she turned it down.

The car felt like it was spinning around them, and she was getting worried her parents would be able to smell what was already on her breath. What she was absolutely certain of is that in the throes of their making out he told her, "*You know what would be fun?*" The details of the next part aren't for the entire world to know-and even if they were, she still would never know them all herself because it seemed as if her body and mind agreed that it was best to forget it all rather than relive the shame of her indiscretion.

    In less time than she could have ever expected, Willow was stumbling out of the short car and trying to correct her sloppily reapplied clothing. She'd had to force her way out, because he did everything he could to keep her from leaving. When she refused to engage anymore, he gripped her arm tightly and told her not to be a bitch. When she heard that word, Willow let that inner voice take over and she listened as it told her to bolt. She looked at his face one last time to memorize it, so she at least had a chance of remembering something, even if it was just what he looked like.

    She kicked at and told him to leave her alone and was afraid he was going to really hurt her. Before he could catch her shirt sleeve tight enough to hold her, his phone rang. He looked at it and answered. She could hear the high-pitched voice of his friend from earlier.

"Aaron, what the hell, where are you?" Although she was confused about him being called another name, she didn't care what it meant since that was her chance to escape and she wasn't missing it. Before he could pull the key fob out of his pocket to lock the door, she kicked it open and ran the best she could without stopping.

Her entire body felt weird, and she realized she wasn't wearing her tights anymore, but it was too late to worry about that since she was due on the bus any second now and she couldn't chance him catching up with her. Her stomach jumped violently, and she found herself hiding around a corner as she vomited more than ever before in her life. She caught a glimpse of herself in a large, mirrored window of the venue as she walked by and smoothed her hair down and wiped away some smudges of mascara. Willow stared at her own image with confusion, somehow failing to find herself in the eyes looking back. Turning toward the partition that sectioned the crowd from the crew, she slipped behind it and flashed her backstage pass as her phone lit up again.

Willow met her mom's concerned gaze as she walked up and realized instantly that she was in deep trouble. Her Mom's blonde curls bounced as her head whipped around and her green eyes blazed with anger. "Willow Dawn, we need to talk. Bus. Now!"

She followed the direction of her mother's shaking finger, straight to the tour bus that already held her Dad and J. As soon as she stepped aboard, her dad got a weird look on his face and her mom slammed the door behind her and dropped the heavy merch box onto the couch. She didn't even need to say it because J beat her to the punch.

"Whoa, skunk! Whoa stinks." His shorthand name for Willow (Whoa) coupled with the revelation that they had all come to was a damning statement. Her Dad stared at her and she fought to meet his gaze and couldn't. Her eyes felt heavy, and her head was pounding, but mostly she was ashamed of what she prayed they didn't know. Her Dad was pissed, but it was her mom that spoke her fate.

"Willow, this is the last show you go out on your own. I don't know who you were with that smokes weed but you were certainly up to more than you led us to believe. We should have known better. This is our fault, too." She looked at her husband with tears in her eyes. "Max she's fourteen and she's high as a tightrope at a circus. We should have known... she's just a kid still." His silence still spoke volumes and Willow felt herself shrinking with every word left unspoken. J began swaying and humming and then he screeched loudly and screamed, "Whoa okay? Whoa?"

Her Dad asked him to start counting and they did deep breathing. He patted J on the back and said, "It's okay Jordan she's with us now. Willow's safe."

J ran to his nook of the bus they had set up especially for decompression. She heard him crawl under his weighted blanket and soon give a little giggle. She kept her eyes closed and was met with the occasional red or pink flash across her blank brain canvas. She was dizzy, miserable, and tried to remember what she had just done, but already it was fading away. All Willow could hear was a haunting echo asking the question that she wished she would have tried harder to say no to. *"You know what would be fun?"* It chased her into all corners of her mind as she tried to escape.

The pursuit was interrupted by her dad's sternest scream whisper. "Willow, I asked you a question and I expect a damn answer!" She sat up with confusion and he could tell she hadn't heard him, so he repeated with anger and disappointment, "Young lady I said-*who was he?*" She looked down at her bare legs that should have been covered in the ripped black tights that her mom had giggled over her trying to stumble into before the show. Her denim skirt was twisted, and her legs were pink with cold. Willow stared at her mom who she knew had noticed as she had faded out and was now actively crying but attempting to keep it silent so J didn't get triggered again.

Ror raised her eyebrows and nudged her on angrily, "Answer your father."

Willow's head hung and she whispered the saddest truth of her life so far. Tears overcame her intoxication and embarrassment as she admitted, "I don't know."

♥

Willow's childhood was anything but normal. I know, you've seen this movie before, right? But really there's not much about being on tour half the year that is typical for a growing kid. She was born into an unusual family and from the beginning it was just her mom, dad, J, and herself. If you haven't put the pieces together quite yet, I should clarify that J is better known as Jordan, or the infamous Jordan Blue if you happen to be a fan. The year Willow made her debut is when his career really took off. We're not talking a slow rise to casual celebrity status; it was more like a rocket to the moon. Yes, it was as dramatic as it sounds, some real Hollywood dreams kind of stuff. As happy as she was for his success, Willow was also glad she wasn't old enough to remember the chaos of those first few years.

She took her first steps in an RV park where they had set up for a few days during Jordan's first headlining tour. It was in that same fifth wheel trailer that she spoke her first word, (or letter technically), J. It always seemed fitting to keep the nickname since it was how her Uncle Jordan had always referred to himself when it came to his title with her.

Her Dad loved to tell the story of how J told them Ror was pregnant and how they didn't believe him. When her mom vomited for the third time that day she went to the store and got a test which initially was negative.

Ror picked it up off the counter to throw it away and just as she was about to toss it in the garbage, she saw a flash of pink that hadn't been there before. She held it up to her face so close she could smell her urine soaked into it but couldn't bear to force it away from her eyes-because it was positive.

They had had some issues with infertility, or at least that's what Willow always assumed since all they'd said was that her mom wasn't supposed to be able to have kids and her dad knew that before they got married. Considering Willow was a total surprise, they had some fun with telling their family about her. Jordan had already suspected it, so he was the only one they came straight out and told, "Jordan, Ror is pregnant, you were right. You're going to be an uncle to our baby!" Her Dad always smiled when they reminisced about the reaction they received from him. "Unc J! Baby Ror Max!" He had danced in circles and laughed until he had to sway to regain his balance and composure.

Willow's Grandma Char was really the only other one around back then since Ror's mother Dolores had passed away the year before. So, for Max's Mom, they wanted the perfect reveal. The three of them went to her place for Saturday supper and as they sat around the fire pit and drank pop, Ror asked Char what she was doing the following weekend.

She didn't have plans and patted Ror on the knee and winked. "Why, you just gotta get you some time with the greatest Mama-in-law around?" She chuckled to herself.

Ror looked at her husband and smiled with the reflection of the flames dancing in her green eyes. Max piped up quietly and was afraid the tears would spill out before his words. "Actually, you're going to have to add on to your honored title now, Mom…" He put his hand on Ror's stomach where Willow had begun to take root and his mother's eyes fixed on it. Ror pulled the urine-stained test out of her sweatshirt pocket and handed it to Char without an ounce of shame. With the other hand she grasped the knee that began to shake as Char processed what she had been given. Ror looked her in the eyes and smiled again, "We were hoping you could help us pick out the crib. We've never done this before, and it just seems like a grandma would know best."

♥

Elijah Ellingson's beginning wasn't as celebrated, at least not at first.

Willow came home from the February tour grounded for what may as well have been the rest of eternity. She'd been put on lockdown after her night of poor judgment and was only allowed to talk to her best friend Taylor (better known as Tay) on the phone for fifteen minutes a day, and it was only because her parents knew she needed a friend as much as she needed punishment to reflect on what she'd done (or at least what they knew of what had happened). But when her moping around the house became unbearable, she was cleared for a couple of hours a week with her best friend, with the agreement to regular phone check ins and an aggressive threat of further grounding if there was even the whiff of a boy in her midst.

But what no one realized for a few weeks was that Willow's actions were of their own consequence. It started with a new obsession with corn dogs that she had a hard time completely satisfying. On their way to get Tay a slushie the first time they got to be reunited, she picked up a couple and ate them with the hot salsa she suddenly had the urge to smother them in. Tay wrinkled her nose and took a long pull on her frozen sugar bomb and said honestly, "You're so gross...."

Willow looked at the fried atrocity she was wolfing down and tried to make an excuse, but shrugged instead as if to say, "I know but what can I do."

She tossed the munched sticks left over from her horrid feast and stole Tay's hat. She put it on backwards like her dad wore his as Tay began talking. "Alright, you can do this. I'll head to the park now in case your parents drive by, and you text me the second-the *second* you are done, okay?" Tay hugged Willow tightly as she concluded their plan, which was more of a one-step play in a stupid scheme. Willow hugged her back and began to sob, partly because she loved her so much for not making her face it alone, and mostly because she was terrified about what she was about to do.

It smelled like an elementary school in there. The white walls seemed more blinding against the disgusting false lights that shone down on her with judgment. She could almost feel the clowns in the pictures on the wall laughing at her stupidity. Staring at one with triangles above and below its dinky eyes and an overpainted smile, Willow could swear she heard him mocking, "*Hey kid, you know what would be fun? Know what would be fun! It's not so fun now, is it?!*" She tore her gaze away and searched with a sudden urgency for a toilet.

It was the first time she'd vomited with the whole thing and based on what Tay had said about her mom's pregnancy, it didn't sound like it was getting better anytime soon. The room spun around, and Willow felt like she could sleep for three days straight. She had dealt with the tiredness and constant headaches, but this was the cherry on the whole crap sundae.

After she cleaned up a little, she heard something familiar coming from the lobby. "Willow? Willow Ellingson?" She rushed out to find a pudgy little lady with a red folder in her hand. She raised her hand weakly. "Yeah, that's me. Hi. I'm uh," her stomach lurched again, and she looked at the woman with wide eyes. "Go, go, get to the bathroom. I'll be right here. Pee in a cup while you're in there, too and write your name on it." She rushed back to the single stall toilet, tossed out the rest of her corn dogs, did as she was told and repeated the wash up routine before returning to the lobby. "Better?" The lady asked, and Willow nodded.

They weighed her before they went into a little room with teddy bears painted on the wall. Willow was caught between thinking how weird it was to be carrying a child while still seeing a children's doctor, and the fact that she had gained more than five pounds in the last couple of weeks. The nurse asked her a few questions about the reason for her visit and she wasn't sure what to say, so she said nothing.

She just stared at the floor and wondered what the odds were that her parents would be arriving any moment. Just as the water works started up again, she felt a cold hand grasp hers.

"Willow, I don't know your story. What I do know is that you are not old enough to make big choices about what I think you might be here for-at least not without your parents. I know that's scary." She squatted down to eye level so they were equals. "Trust me," she said with a painful whisper, "I know because I've been there, and you are not alone. You are going to make it through this, no matter what you decide to do." Willow's heart hurt already from facing the reality of what she'd done and felt like it was trying to run away from her. She lay back and closed her eyes and gently nodded her head in a silent surrender to beckon her parents.

The nurse dropped her hand with a squeeze and checked Willow's blood pressure and all the other stuff they do in a doctor's office when you get there. While she wrote it all down Willow asked, "How did you know anyway? When I called I said I had allergies." They looked at one another and the nurse smiled slightly. She said, "Well kid, I've never seen allergies make someone puke like that. Like I said, I've been there and once you're a mom you can spot a Mama to be from a mile away."

*Oh God, am I a mom?* Willow thought with a new kind of queasiness. That felt different in her gut to think about; it was the first time she'd realized that it was happening-not a conversation with Tay or a scary thought, but a reality she had to deal with. Thankfully, she was already laying down because she was getting dizzy.

"I'm going to call your mom and when she gets here, Dr. Miller will come see you, too, okay?" Willow muttered something agreeable and covered her eyes with her hands. *Goddammit shit fuck bitch asshole!* She cussed a silent nonsensical blue streak thinking it might act as a bloodletting for her fear, but it provided her no relief. Suddenly she was so scared. As ashamed and angry as she was with herself, she wished she could deny that all that she wanted was her mom to be there anyway.

While she waited, Willow memorized the patterns in the holes of the ceiling above her and the scratches around the handles of the drawers on the counter. She searched for anything to distract her from what was to come but within twenty minutes she heard a quiet rap on the door before Ror gracefully entered the room with Max and Tay trailing behind. She groaned with embarrassment and relief. Before she could say more, a short old man in a perfectly creased white lab coat entered the room. He looked mean and Willow sat up.

"Well, apparently we're doing this family style today," he said as he looked around the packed room. He continued in a tired voice, "Look, Willow, from what I understand your friend here has filled your parents in-who told *me*-so we all know why we are here. The urine test you left did confirm, you are pregnant. Now, the question is what do you do about it?"

She was far too entrenched in guilt to look at anyone, so she found a scratch in the linoleum and focused on that. It was long and deep and not boring holes into her with accusing eyes. He continued by explaining that based on the date of her last period (which her mom gave him-ew!), she was about six weeks along. He just told everyone she loved that she was *pregnant*. Willow let it soak in and felt the shame building and she thought, *I'm such a slut, God I'm such a screw up....*

There was no stopping the tears now and a little puddle formed between her feet and filled the scratch on the floor. Suddenly she felt arms slide around her and a big hand gently lean her head against a shoulder that felt like home. Dad.

"I'm so sorry, I'm so sorry, I'm..." He just hugged her tighter and said, "Shhhh, it's gonna be ok, kid."

Her Mom kneeled onto the floor in front of her, grabbed Willow's hands and gently asked the doctor to give them a minute. Tay tried to slip out with him, but her mom said firmly but softly, "Nope. She needs you, hon. Hang tight."

Willow scooted closer to Max and perched her head against the top of his shoulder and squeezed Ror's hands. She looked up and saw Tay standing there with tears streaming down her own face. All she could say is, "Sorry Will, they made me tell..." Willow looked to her mom for answers, advice, or really anything at all. What she said made her think that everything might be all right after all. "Baby, you don't have to make any choices right now. And don't think for a second we aren't having the longest talk of your life sometime soon. But before that you need to decide what you are going to do. No matter what you choose your life is going to be turned upside down and there's no getting around it. But I'm not making this choice for you. You got yourself here and now you get to choose what direction to take your future, and the future of the baby inside of you."

They all instinctively looked down and Willow's hand gravitated below her belly button. She nodded as tears continued to stream down her face, dizzy and more tired than when she walked in there.

She freed her hands and gently hit them onto the exam table with a sigh. Her Dad kissed the top of her head and Dr. Miller walked back in.

"Okay guys, I hate to rush you out of here, but I have a very grumpy four-year-old in the lobby with an earache." He met Max's gaze on the childish imagery on the walls around them. "As you can imagine, pregnancy isn't something we deal with every day here, but I asked Judy to get me some information while you were talking..." He went to hand them to Ror and forced himself to shift his hand in Willow's direction, full of pamphlets with words she hadn't even considered yet. "There are some valuable resources here in Avery and if need be, they have more advanced...*care*...in Boris."

He was doing that try to smile and show disapproval at the same time thing, and he shook Max's hand and patted Ror on the shoulder on his way out. "Good luck to you. Willow, I assume I'll see you when you need a pediatrician again." She thanked him and waved limply. As she stood up, she got a little lightheaded again. When she stepped forward, Willow felt the strength of Tay's arm around her waist as they walked forward together, and somehow it was as if they didn't carry the weight of everything between their narrow shoulders.

♥

Back home, she was feeling weaker yet. They dropped Tay off at home just in time to watch her little sister so her mom could get to work at the gas station. She hugged Willow hard and quietly said to text her if she needed to face chat that night. Willow found herself lying on the quilt J let her borrow and wishing she knew what the hell she was supposed to do. Her Dad knocked and sat next to her. Glancing at his face, she realized he looked really old that day. Every time she'd see him, she was overcome with a sense of guilt. Not the kind you get if you think you might pull a crappy grade, but the kind that sinks deep into your soul-like wearing a wet set of clothing and not being able to change.

    He didn't hug her this time but instead looked around her room. Willow saw him glancing at the pictures she had everywhere, moments frozen with smiles and laughter. He spoke gently, "Wow. It never occurred to me that by doing road school, you'd never really have things like participation trophies or spelling bee prizes-even if they seem lame. Your life hasn't been real normal, kid. Until now I wasn't sorry for that, but I'm starting to see that our choice to go on the road for so long was so selfish... I'm sorry Willow. I mean, you're in deep shit for sure-but I'm not blaming it solely on you. And, for the record, we love you so much and this... baby, doesn't change that. But kid, you've got a hard choice to make like your mom said."

"We can't do that for you, but you need to think about your future. What do you want your life to look like in eighteen years? You will be thirty-three. Do you want to be going to your kid's graduation, or do you have other plans for your life? Do you think someone else could raise your baby and love it as their own so that you can have all the opportunities that you deserve as a young teenager? Would you be able to let go of a baby if you carried it for nine months?"

He sighed. "That's so much to think about, ugh. But we need to open the conversation now. Mom and I talked about it and because you are early in the pregnancy you still have all options on the table. We feel strongly about what we think you should do, but we want you to think it over and talk to us about it at dinner. Obviously, you don't need to make a final decision now because we don't want you to rush-this is a life we are talking about. But we want to start the first of many family talks about this together tonight."

She just sat there staring at her wall that held no evidence of a normal childhood and thought about how she had never known anything else. Not only that, but how had this never once occurred to her? There she was, a fourteen-year young roadie that had been given opportunities that even most adults would never have.

Who has met all their favorite bands and seen them play live, and knew some of their kids? She had. Yes, she was from a small and painfully traditional town but her life had fallen short of reflecting that in any way but her slight country dialect and ignorant naiveté.

As she often found a need to do, Willow forced her mind to quiet with a full rotation of the ring her Grandma Char had given her. The slipping of the cool metal around her finger was always enough to shift her train of thought and it worked then, too. One thought escaped into the air before she could stop it. "Dad, I can't be a mom..." Just hearing the sentence with herself in the place of a parent's rightful position seemed so off, and she looked at him as the tears fell. She began to feel younger with every moment that hung upon the walls of her room and stared back at her. "Dad, I don't even know how to do algebra, or cook, or anything about laundry, or life, really. How can I raise a baby? I can't do it.... But also," She looked down and massaged her bloaty tummy with both hands over her sweatshirt, "I can't do *it* either. I know what abortion is, kind of? I can't kill my baby; I won't do it. Yuck, I have a baby though! What do I do?!"

Willow was sobbing and for once she thought Max might be at a complete loss as to what advice to offer. He was silent as she realized the rawness of the situation she had allowed herself to get into.

Before he got up to leave, she heard the door squeak open and her mom float softly into the room. Willow looked at her through heavy, blurred eyes. Ror patted Max on the shoulder as a signal to end his vigil as she took his place next to Willow. Her hands fell over her daughter's which were now shaking over her stomach. "Hon, it's been a long day. I know you have a lot to think about, but I have something to share that might help in your decision. It doesn't have to be now; when you're ready, we can go out to my tree and I'll tell you all about it. But for now, I'm just here. I love you."

    She put her head on Willow's shoulder and heard the release of what was left in her daughter's exhausted little reserve of will. Willow nodded, using up her mom's beautiful golden curls to absorb her snot and salty tears. She whispered the only thing at that moment she knew she could be sure of, "I love you too Mom. Thank you for not hating me for this."

♥

The sky was grumbling as Willow peeked out at the smooth gray sheet heaving with water. She knew it would be a minute before Ror was ready to meet her there, so Willow waited, and drank in the smell of a gentle impending storm. The goats were still gnawing at the grass and tree bark and seemed to not care or realize that they were about to get soaked. Across the pasture the flock of chickens was rushing inside the coop to roost-they were nobody's dummies! Their heeler Emmy gave a little woof and headed in the house to look for J. She may have been a champion gopher hunter, but she wasn't much for bravery against mother nature.

Without even looking, she could suddenly hear Ror settling on the ground beside her. Ever since Willow could remember, her mom had come out there when she needed alone time. She said it was her God tree and Willow always thought that was cool even though it was a little cheesy. Lately the idea of God existing at all seemed farfetched to her pregnant child's mind, but she put that aside for the time being out of respect for the sacred space they occupied out where wild came to meet their land. Willow looked out at the field edged with mountains that built in layers; just seeing them seemed to put her at ease a little bit.

The land she called home was nothing particularly special but there was a silent majesty about it that Willow just needed sometimes, something she learned to crave from her mom. On the windy days when she sat below it, invisible gusts would rattle the aspen and shake it's leaves as Ror would look out, like Willow was now-at nothing but kind of everything, too. A couple times Willow had asked her dad about it (since she didn't know if it was normal for a mom to chill under a tree alone while her family was off doing their own thing). His response had been a thoughtful grin and a weird statement to the effect of her visiting an old friend. It was dorky enough for Willow to be disinterested almost instantly, so she let them have their God tree (whatever that meant) and figured maybe one day she'd be let in on the big secret.

And here they were. She guessed she had to join the Mom Club or something, but whatever the reason, she had arrived. Willow sat against the peely white bark that was nice and smooth, for a tree. Looking up she could see the heavy gray sky as it highlighted the lime green of the budded branches. The tiny leaves began to rattle and they were treated to an infantile quaking sound.

Willow was transfixed with the patterns in the branches and her mom scooched in close and offered her arm, like a mother hen swooping a chick underneath her wing. Willow may have been a teenager (and may also have been pregnant), but she was also very much a kid as well. She accepted and scooted in at an angle so her head lay on the smooth place between her mom's collarbone and shoulder. Ror squeezed Willow tightly.

"Come here, I'll keep you warm. I'm glad to see you're not entirely too cool for your lame old Mom..." Willow sighed. "Alright sorry, cheese, I know-we've been over this. Anyway, thanks for hanging out with me here. There's so much about a little patch of grass under a tree that I have wanted to share with you your entire life. This spot is special, hon." She began to gaze at a lightning strike far off in the distance, reaching its finger to touch a hill at least ten miles away. "Looks like this storm is coming to us sooner than later though so I'm going to make this kind of brief. Are you cool with just listening for a minute?" Willow nodded, curious about what she was about to hear.

A little shiver ran through Willow's spine as her mom told her about being about six years older than Willow was then and moving to Avery from Oklahoma- which she had never heard before.

Ror then asked something that perked her ears up especially. "Remember how Dad and I said we weren't supposed to be able to have kids, but then we got to have you? Well, that was something I knew before I met Dad. I was married before, I was forced to be, when I was sixteen...." Willow looked over at her mom's face as her perfectly arched eyebrows raised, and she looked back at her intensely.

"Yeah, it was awful. You don't need the details-not because you're young, but because it's stuff you can never unhear. What I will say is that the only purpose I served for that man was to create kids and my body could not do it. And he beat the hell out of me for it." Willow gasped and Ror patted her arm gently. "I'm okay hon. What I wanted to say was that God didn't want me to have a kid. Not with him, not like that. When your dad and I got together, we did the corny Christian thing and didn't have sex 'til our wedding night but it sure didn't take long to make you. I was married to the monster for four years and never conceived but within a year of my marriage with your dad-this incredible man-I was sicker than a dog with morning sickness and happy to tears. I don't know how God works or why and I never will. What I do know is that sometimes the big picture is so much greater than we have the capacity to see in the moment. Do you understand what I'm saying Willow?"

She shrugged and nervously absorbed the thunder that rumbled overhead. They both silently counted the eight seconds that followed and watched the lightning hit as many miles away, this time to the east. "What I'm trying to say is that the map for your kid's life is written. You can't see it any more than any of us can, but even if you don't feel like you're equipped to help them navigate their journey, there may be someone-or a couple of someones-that are. Only you can decide what to do and in time you will know for certain. I brought you out here because your grandma used to tell me that God is everywhere, and she had trees out back here just waiting for us to sit under and talk to Him. This one has always been where He and I meet, so I wanted to introduce you. It's my God tree."

Just then a great tear traveled along the sky above and they both screamed and booked it for the house as fast as they could. Willow slammed the back door just as another rumble fell and a torrential downpour covered the hungry Earth. She took another look at her mom and laughed. "God Mom, that was pretty dramatic. Did we have to get so close to dying for you to tell me you think I should adopt him out?"

Suddenly they paused and instinctively looked at Willow's stomach. Ror smiled sweetly and Willow touched her itty-bitty bump without thinking. "You think it's a boy, huh?"

She looked out at the tree and got a chill, discounting her mom's comment and focusing on something she couldn't quite describe.

"Do you see this? Mom what is that?" She hurried over to the kitchen window and heard Ror giggle as she gazed upon a red streak as it moved slowly from the aspen tree and off into the field. Willow looked at her with wide eyes and before she could stammer out another word, Ror got a huge smile on her face and they watched the thing together. With a sad pride she said, "That Willow, is your grandma Dolores. She's not a ghost or anything creepy but sometimes she seems to just want to be here for the big stuff. Last time I saw something like that was the day I brought you home from the hospital."

Willow was completely creeped out and continued to hold her tummy as she wiggled her anxiety out. Her Mom explained, "For real, it's nothing negative. We buried her under the God Tree because it was special to us. She belongs here and I think that as she looks down on us, she likes to let us know she's still a part of the family." On this last word she choked, and Willow hugged her even though the whole conversation had been extremely weird. "Sorry Willow, not trying to freak you out. The weather isn't helping the vibe, either. I just miss her, that's all. Anyway, I'm hungry. You?"

Willow nodded dramatically, grateful for a distraction from the eerie conversation. "What for?" Ror asked as she turned for the fridge. Without hesitation the pregnant teen gushed a sudden unmistakable craving. "Two corn dogs with super-hot salsa!" J and Dad laughed from the living room, and she could see J begin doing some funky dance moves as he screamed with joy. He always liked strange meals and Willow had a feeling he was in for a treat the next several months as the baby kept drawing her closer to the greasy and hot side of the menu.

She looked down at him and thought about how he was a person as well as a little bump, and the kid just wanted some corn dogs. She sighed with exhaustion. "Why not? Corn dogs and salsa are no weirder than Grandma buried in the back yard and visiting from the grave. You can have all you want bud." She patted her tummy and headed into the family room as she thought about how normal it was to be so extraordinarily strange in her family. Walking into the yellow lit room and a dance party held by her three favorite people, she couldn't help but shake her head and smile a little as she thought, *If weird is the worst he is, this kid is going to be okay. We are both going to be fine, no matter what.*

♥

She had always liked how the world zips by when you're on the road. Spring Break was an upheaval of everyone's life, and Willow was relieved to escape it and return to her second home, which happened to be: everywhere. Opening night, J had a show in Boise of all places. They had left the night before, after the hardest goodbye she'd ever had with Tay. They had just sat there on Tay's doorstep and laughed at her little sister who was dancing in her little toddler awkwardness. Tay told Willow about her new schedule that term and how she was excited about her advanced math class, but not health. Willow was excited for her because Lydia, their mutual friend, was also in world history so she hoped at least that would dull the boredom a little.

When Max pulled up in the RV, J came bursting out the door so he could dance with little Olivia. Tay instinctively moved to pick her up, but Willow touched her arm to let her know it was okay. She relaxed as they both watched him stop several feet from the baby and match her rhythm perfectly, bobbing back and forth with his head as his hips and knees swayed along. It was goofy but cute and Willow looked up to find her dad leaning against the RV with a smirk, also amused by his friend who was anything but usual. Olivia just watched J with awe and squealed whenever he copied her silly moves.

When the moment passed J just said, "K bye," and skipped back onto the bus as Max waved and told them hello. "Hey girls, it's about that time. I'll wait inside. Taylor, be good and have fun at school. We'll catch you next time we're in town." He turned to get into the driver's side but paused and said gently, "Thanks kid, for being there this week. You're Dad and I hung out yesterday and I let him know how much we appreciate you, especially right now." Tay's Dad wasn't exactly a present father, being single and working a lot, but he and Max had a drink every now and again to catch up. Willow always wondered if it wasn't just a way for her dad to keep him up to date on important stuff as it happened but figured there was some actual guys hang time in there too.

Tay waved back at him. "Thanks Mr. Ellingson. Yeah, Dad told me. It's no big deal, it's what friends are for." This he took as his cue to leave, and the girls were left there to corral Olivia so Tay could prop the toddler onto her non-existent hip. Willow threw her arms around them both. Tay just held her until the little one started to get grumpy, which wasn't long. Willow stepped back, and Tay's eyes got wide as she handed Olivia over. "Dude, I almost forgot! Hold her, I need to get something."

She ran into the house and was back in a matter of seconds.

It was barely enough time for Willow to rest her nose on the child's soft hair and memorize the smell of the gentle shampoo her mom had used on her pokey strands. People were right, that smell is like an addiction. For anyone else it would be borderline creepy, but with her maternal hormones in full swing it made her so incredibly aware that she had one of those in her own tummy. She looked curiously at her bestie as she ran out of the house and jumped the two steps down to the walkway where Willow stood. She grabbed Olivia and then presented a clenched fist which she opened excitedly. In it was a colorful bracelet of pink, blue, and red. She motioned Willow over and managed to secure it to her left wrist while still properly holding the baby. As she did so, Willow noticed that she was already wearing hers.

"These aren't just bracelets. They're lifelines. If you're ever having a bad day or miss me, just rub one of the knots and it'll calm you down until we can talk. Never take it off, but if it falls off on its own you have to make a wish. It's the rule." Willow noticed how bright it looked against her now tanned skin and looked back up to find Tay trying to smile. "I love you Will. Everything is going to be okay, and we will talk every night, like always, k?" Willow just nodded and gave her one last hug. Max honked and she turned to the RV before looking back. "Love you too Tay. Thank you for everything."

She put up her pinky and Willow did the same as they meowed once in their secret friendship sign.
Willow waved and forced herself up the stairs of her other home and joined her family for the next journey.

She sat on the couch and looked at the rural chunks of land as they zoomed by. She rubbed the first knot on her bracelet and thought about everything that happened during the week. Willow wished she could just be worried about kid stuff. Her new term of school started the next Monday, and she and her mom were going to do geography, American History, math, and sex ed. Ror had explained that they were going to do the last one the following year, but with Willow's pregnancy, it might be important to visit the subject sooner than later. Considering that she knew nothing about what was going to happen in the next seven months, Willow begrudgingly agreed. At least her dad was going to give her vocal lessons for her arts credit this time. She still needed to get new school supplies which her mom and Dad agreed to as part of the whole helping her feel like a normal student thing, and Willow planned to try to be considerate by keeping it to a cute new pack of pencils and a special notebook-one with a superhero on it if she could find one.

At the current moment, she wasn't really worried about road school or getting cute supplies to normalize it like she always had before. All she could think of was how she didn't know anything, like why she was craving hot corn dogs, who the guy was that had put her in this position, and what she was going to do about it. The next day was the first of April and her mom said that when they got to Boise, she had an appointment to see a real women's pregnancy doctor while J and her dad did soundcheck. Maybe the appointment would help her decide, she hoped so anyway because she was feeling very overwhelmed.

It was raining again, and droplets were flinging onto her window as they escaped from the slick windshield. She focused on one and watched it drip to the windowsill. Without tearing her eyes away, Willow asked simply, "Mom, when is he coming?" Ror pulled the phone away from her ear as Willow heard her ask the person on the line to hold on a moment. With a surprised look, she said quietly, "The uh, the baby? Oh, um," she counted on her fingers quickly and said, "I think late October, or early November." Willow's heart jumped as she realized that it was sooner than she had expected. She just stared at the droplet as it smeared into the corner of the window and more took its place at the top of the glass.

They had another two hours until they pulled into the venue and J was just getting up. Knowing their routine as she did, Willow went to the overhead bin and pulled out the index card ring that was specific to touring. She plopped down next to J and let him touch the tip of her nose with his index finger as he greeted her. "Morn Whoa." Despite all that was running through her head, she couldn't help but smile because she loved her uncle J. "Mornin' J. Got your schedule here if you want to go over it," she told him. He nodded and told her yes before pointing to the first item in the series, identifying that toilet was first, then shower, get dressed, eat at the venue, spins, mic check, and finally perform.

    He saw that she had also grabbed a stack of letters his fans wrote him which Max must have gotten from the PO Box they used for fan mail when they were at home. He pointed to them and said, "A lot!" Willow agreed and asked if J wanted her to read them to him after he used the toilet. He agreed and said, "No poop yet, so okay." She laughed because she knew he was reminding himself not to break the cardinal rule of RV's, especially after they all got to smell the consequences of it for hours on the way to Denver last year when he unloaded a hefty deuce on the bus. He slowly scratched his head and walked to the bathroom a few feet away. While he was in there, Willow could hear him humming and then say loudly, "Baby?"

Suddenly her heart felt like it stopped for a second. She hadn't talked to him about it yet and kind of forgot he just knew that type of stuff. Or he could have heard it from Mom and Dad. Either way, he knew. She responded as breezily as she could. "Oh, like is he doing okay, or what do you mean?" He washed his hands and wiped them on his shorts as he walked toward her. "He okay?" He repeated with earnest. The fact that she was discussing her soon to be child with Uncle J was making it a more concrete reality and she realized the whole thing was pulling in everyone around her like a vacuum, or something.

"Um, I think so. It's still early, I don't know how big he is or anything, but I go to a doctor today to learn more." J looked behind Willow but was trying to make eye contact with her, so she knew he was invested in the conversation. He told her, "Whoa Mama. Weird Whoa. Okay though." He put his hand up for a high five and she met him there. For a brief second, his hand clasped hers in the air and again she heard him reassure her, "Be okay Whoa." She thanked him and smiled.

Pulling out the letters to read to him, Willow counted them quickly. "J you've got thirty-seven this time! This is just from this week though. Might not be able to read them before Boise but let's try. We can work on writing them back tonight as we drive to Salt Lake City."

He began his morning sways, and she opened the first letter which was written in a determined but sloppy scrawl. She could tell already it was written by a child or a person living with disabilities and before she read the words, Willow already loved this person for making such an effort to connect with J. "Mr. Blue, I just want to tell you that you inspire me ..." She began reading it aloud to him and smiled with the first line which she couldn't agree with more. J just giggled and said, "Yes."

♥

*Well,* Willow thought to herself, *that was gross and awkward.* She and Ror had just walked out of the doctor's office, and she couldn't stop thinking about everything she'd just learned. Willow thought with disgust about everything she would soon be dealing with: Trouble pooping, but then peeing all the time, still feeling sick and puking, and apparently getting fat. And you didn't want to get her started on how this kid had to get out of her! She was really upset about that in particular. She was fourteen! Before she got pregnant, she had probably eight periods- and they were so embarrassing! Willow had hated everything about them. Her boobs barely only came in the last year and now they hurt all the time and her doctor said they were going to become living bottles and get bigger, too. It all seemed disgusting.

    Beyond this information overload was the hard conversation that was coming up every time someone found out. They never came out and said things like, *Well are you getting an abortion? Are you going to give him up? Will you be keeping him?* She got it; those are hard things to say to a child (which is what Willow was) but they're what everyone was thinking. The truth was that she'd known the answer since the night of that weird storm.

Even though she didn't know the details about really any of her options until that day, Willow knew that she wanted her kid to have a chance at life. It still pissed her off that for that to happen, she had to do the whole crappy pregnancy thing, but that wasn't the baby's fault. The idea of having one doctor visit and walking out as a kid with no responsibility again was more tempting than anything she had ever faced. In fact, she'd thought about it a lot, even after she already had made her choice. However, she realized that what she was going to do is find someone who was better equipped to raise the baby as their own. He deserved a fighting chance and Willow couldn't give him that at her age. Maybe other girls could, but she was still figuring out life for herself. She could bring the baby on the road with the family and all that, but what kind of life was that for him? A young teenage mom, no dad, and raised in a touring family... kids need stability, and she couldn't give him that, but she was willing to bet there was someone out there who could.

The OB/GYN visit was weird and kind of icky in general, but one thing happened that helped Willow make up her mind for sure about what she would do. The doctor had her lay down and put warm goo on her tummy. Ror sat next to her, and they both looked at the ultrasound screen that had some black and gray static and blobs.

Willow was beginning to wonder what was so exciting about it, but then she saw a little bitty flicker on the screen inside a faint white outline. With wide eyes she looked at the doctor, who turned up the sound and smiled at she and Ror both. A soft whooshing was first and then she heard it, *thump thump, thump thump, thump....* A tiny quick heartbeat stole the floor. It was so beautiful, she wished she could describe it better than that, it was almost...magical. Somehow, she just knew that was the moment she should make it official to her mom, so Willow told her softly. "I already love him, Mom. I can't...you know. But I can't be his mom either. I'm going to search until I find the perfect family."

Ror squeezed her hand and began sobbing as the doctor excused herself. It was the first time her mom had let her see the depth of her emotions about Willow's situation. Willow just looked at her with tears of her own and listened as her mom told her she was so proud of her choice, and so mad that she even had to make it. They agreed to talk to Max that night and thanked the doctor before catching a cab back to the venue. Willow stared out the window silently and thought about the weird day and how many more were yet to come before her life would be normal again. Would it ever be back to normal at all, she wondered?

Before she got too caught up in the tailspin, Willow caught a glimpse of the people gathering for the show. It seemed like a younger crowd than usual, and she looked around curiously at them before ducking into the green room prepped with all of the calming items J included on his rider. He'd gotten his noise canceling headphones on, no doubt listening to some instrumental guitar tracks. She could smell the lavender essential oils vaporized into the air and appreciated that there was as little foot traffic in there as possible.

Willow snatched a vegetable juice and sat down next to her dad, who greeted she and her mom with a hug. He asked how the doctor's appointment went and Willow just grunted and burrowed her head into his chest. Ror patted her on the back and said gently, "It was a pretty big day, but it sounds like we have a plan now." With that, Max rubbed the back of Willow's hair and kissed the top of her head. He got the hint to drop it and told her, "Good. I'm proud of you, kid," and she couldn't help but feel awful about the fact that this is what she'd given her parents to be proud of her for.

For the first time all day, she had the chance to catch her breath. Her parents went over to the corner and talked softly so that she could fall asleep for what seemed like the millionth time in the last couple of months.

Laying her head down on the grungy old couch, Willow tried not to think about how many heads (or other body parts) had laid there before her. She pulled her knees up into her chest and used one of J's extra weighted blankets to soothe herself into slumber. In the middle of a theater bustling with life and excitement, she allowed herself to slip into a hormone laden sleep that lasted until the end of J's set.

♥

The first month of tour flew by more quickly than usual. Willow finally caught the show on night three after she had captured some adequate rest. J upped his game by expanding his setlist and throwing in a cover or two for shock value. Everything sounded better through the filter of his work, and the covers themselves brought forth a roar of glee. Obviously, she took it all in from a different seat, this time beside her mom at the merch booth rather than free range out in the crowd like before. Although it felt less liberating, it was nice to share that moment with her mom each night. As proud as she was of J, the love Ror and Max had for him would always be so much greater. Although Willow sometimes had to do homework during a set or listen to a history lesson on her headphones while she set up the booth, she truly wouldn't change the fact that her academic and otherwise "real" life collided with the professional music world of her awesome uncle.

There were ten more shows before they got to take a long break and then head overseas for one last leg for the year. Her Dad had said this time it was in Australia and Willow couldn't pretend not to be beside herself with excitement because she had never been there and had always wanted to go. That said, it was right in the middle of the most terrifying time of her life, so she figured she'd see how it all played out before she got her heart set on that part of the tour.

Her Mom swore they would be back home at least three weeks before the baby was due and that they should have plenty of time to prepare for him and his family. But at the moment, Willow was getting ready to take her midterm tests. That had to be her focus for a while, that and checking in with Tay regularly because she had a big crush on someone and wouldn't say who yet (but Willow thought it might be James because he was the only cute guy in any of her classes).

    As if that all wasn't enough to juggle, she had been flipping through some binders her parents had picked up from three different adoption agencies. You know, just trying to pick a family to raise and keep her child forever, typical kid stuff. Really though, she had no idea how to choose something like that. Does someone's job have anything to do with what kind of parent they will be? Does their religion? Or the fact that they're gay or straight, or single? Willow wished more than anything that she knew the answers because so far, she had about a dozen different options that she'd become attached to. One was a doctor, another a teacher. There was a gay couple who seemed like they'd be hip and kind of fun. One woman was a single lady that had her own non-profit organization helping homeless people off the street.

Another reminded her of Grandma Char and had worked hard labor all her life but seemed to have a similar no-nonsense, all-love take on life.

They all had great aspects that seemed would make them great parents, including most of them already having children of their own. But she had to agree with what Tay had told her-anyone can write great things about themselves, but your gut doesn't lie about how to feel about a person. Her mom said that was intuition, and considering she was in this position in the first place, Willow wasn't sure she should trust her own. But luckily, she wasn't in it alone. The plan was to continue her monthly doctor appointments and once she reached about five months or so, she would start meeting the families in person. It made her feel the nervous diarrhea coming on just thinking about it, but she knew it was important.

As her stomach stretched a tiny bit at a time, Willow's vomiting seemed to be getting a little less frequent. Her head hurt a lot of the time and she swore she'd never been so hungry. Thankfully, the salsa dogs had started being replaced by a constant need to eat broccoli and hummus. Her dad thought her body was needing iron, and Willow had a feeling after November she'd never be eating corn dogs or broccoli again. But for the time being, it worked.

Willow and J had been on walks every day, usually going around the block wherever they ended up staying for the night. They tried to keep him disguised as well as they could and only once did paparazzi trail them. Willow found that out only because she saw the two of them in the paper the next day with a headline that read, "Famed autist Jordan Blue out on the town with mystery girl in Des Moines." The family got a kick out of the whole thing and was grateful that Willow happened to be wearing one of her dad's sweatshirts and a ball cap so they couldn't see her bump. That kind of discovery would have been sure to stir up the hornets' nest!

Nothing about the tour had been normal and they all felt it. There were darker circles under everyone's eyes and more naps where there would normally be singing and goofy conversation. Even J seemed more subdued in some sense.

One night they were in Cincinnati and Max texted Willow from the venue where they were setting up. He said that after she and Ror grabbed some grub for everyone that he had a surprise for her. Willow's heart skipped a little as she read her phone because she was excited at the prospect of breaking the mold of the road grind. She was ready to shake the dust a little and do something- anything.

She thought about the day her dad found out about the baby and what his face was like as he looked around and realized what a strange life Willow had led as a kid. Since then, he'd stuck a little closer and been a little more available. Not that he had ever been absent or anything, but he just was checking in with her more. It would annoy most kids, but with all the wacked out stuff she was feeling all the time, it was nice just to have her dad there when she needed him the most.

Willow texted back, asking him what she should wear, and he sent her the shrugging shoulders emoji and then told her just to be comfy. His sign off was on brand but right then she appreciated it more than usual. "See you soon kid, sure do love you." She smiled to herself as she rifled around the overhead bin and dug out her black sweatshirt. When she pulled on some red skinny jeans and fastened the hairband that had been rigged to replace the buttonhole, Willow turned around to see her mom grabbing her purse.

"You look cute, hon. Where do you think you're going?" Willow rolled her eyes, knowing she was just joking. "Very funny. WE are going to get pizza, Dad said he already told you!" She smiled and hugged Ror. "I know," her mom said, "I just wanted to see you sweat for a second." Willow giggled and melted into her mother's warmth. "Fair enough."

"By the way, I think the baby wants Hawaiian pizza... he's had me craving pineapple ever since I read the word 'food.'" Ror wrinkled her nose in disapproval. "Yuck. We're gonna have to teach that kid to have better taste before he gets here." Willow laughed and found her hand hovering lightly over her tummy where it seemed livelier lately. She thought about how weird it was that her hand was out in the world but also touching the house of a little person growing inside her. *God*, she thought for the millionth time that week, *I have another person being made inside of my body...*

    While they walked down the road to the pizza joint she'd scoped out online, Willow tried to find the words she didn't quite know how to say. "Mom, what if he grows up and he hates me?" Ror looked at her with a furrowed brow and grabbed her hand and stopped walking. "Willow, why would you ever think your kid would hate you?" She felt the tears rolling (again). "I don't know, what if he hates the family that raises him and spends his whole childhood wishing he knew me? Even worse, what if he meets me and he's glad I'm not his family? Mom, does it mean I don't love him if I can't raise him? I love him Mom, I do, so much!"

    Willow was on her knees now and was sobbing into her mom's chest as Ror held her on the sidewalk.

Strangers passed and she was sure they whispered as they wondered what was going on. Ror smoothed her daughter's hair and gently held her small face in her hands.

She looked straight into Willow's dripping eyes and asked her, "Honey, can you give him everything he deserves as he grows up?" Willow just blubbered more and shook her head. "Do you feel like you are prepared to be the mother he deserves?" Again, her head signaled a no. "Willow, what you are going through is probably the hardest thing you will ever face. But you created life, and I'm so proud of you for taking care of him in the way you can; only you can raise this baby in your body. I wish this didn't happen at this time in your life, trust me, but you are his Mama and finding him a family that is able to give him the life that you can't as a fourteen-year-old is the most loving gift you can give. Will he hate you? Baby I can't say for sure. What I can tell you is that you will never forget this love you have for him and why you made the choice you did."

Willow felt so tiny and young, like she'd just fallen on the playground and needed to hear her mom say she was going to be fine and should go play again. She was not ready to stand in Ror's shoes, to be the one to tell her baby that it was all going to be okay.

Her Mom was right, she was not ready for any of this at all. Her gut knew it, and her heart did too.

She felt a weird little flutter in her tummy she didn't recognize and looked up at her mom in surprise. Without thinking she pulled her hand down and put it where the feeling came from. Ror smiled and nuzzled her daughter's dark hair. "He must support you more than you thought hon, this is what it feels like when your baby kicks. You'll never ever forget that, either."

Ror helped Willow rise to a stand, and they walked the rest of the short distance like any other mother and daughter. As they walked into the pizzeria, Willow inhaled the cheesy garlic exhaust in the air and felt another flutter. As Ror picked up their order, she rubbed her belly and smirked to herself as she thought, *well, starting off in the world with a love for pizza is as good a place to start as any.*

♥

Max had a cab sitting curbside and opened the door for Willow to slide in. She scooched over to the far side as he got in after her. When she saw that they'd settled in, the older pink haired lady who was driving took off in a tear. Willow looked at her dad and tried to inexplicably ask him if he should tell the driver where to go. He just smiled, and the lady's gravelly smoker's voice cut in sharply, "I got you kid-just sit back and relax!" Willow looked again at Max, and he couldn't help but laugh at the fact that for once he'd kept something a surprise from her.

"Whatever we're doing, thank you. It's nice to get away from the bus and as much as I love everyone…" He finished the sentence for her, "Being with them so much is enough to drive you freaking crazy." Willow laughed. "Yep, exactly." Max sighed and stretched as much as the old cab would allow, splaying out his arms and clasping his hands behind his head. "I know. If I had to go over Jordan's intro one more time today, I was going to lose it. For some reason, the light techs were really struggling. Was about to climb up there myself." He looked out the window and let out another sigh. "Anyway, the point of this is to escape all that for a bit. Mom wanted to do pizza with Jordan tonight so I figured this would be a good gig. I've always wondered what it was like."

Willow had been so focused on what he was saying that she didn't realize that their driver had swung onto the final exit before their destination. As they drove under the enormous freeway sign, she read, "Zoo, 1 mile" and looked to her dad excitedly. In all the crazy adventures her life had held, a trip to a zoo had never been one of them. All she could do was squeal and hug him. He laughed again, which was a sound Willow was glad to be hearing so often that day. "I know right?!" He explained, "My Dad always said he wanted to take me, but he never had the chance. Figure you're never too old to go to the zoo with your old man... or grandpa, too. Guess today is a two-fer, huh?"

They both looked at the bump that was now poorly concealed by clothing, a tiny mountain rising out of her childish body. She felt all sorts of things and didn't know how to respond so Willow just smiled and then looked out the window. Suddenly the driver announced loudly, "Alright, here we are! Now get out of here you crazy kids. Max, that'll be forty buckeroos. Be sure to see the walrus he's a real hoot."

As she drove away, Max and Willow looked after the car. She shook her head, and he pinched the spot between her shoulder and neck and laughed. "She's kinda weird, isn't she?" He asked. Willow nodded in agreement and said she liked the strange lady.

As the car squealed around the corner and disappeared, Max replied in an amused voice, "Yeah, I know. Me too."

♥

They were on the road again already. Between the trip with her dad, the emotional pizza retrieval with her mom, and of course J's show, Willow was completely wiped out. All she wanted was to crash hard and let the road lull her into dreams of home where there was quiet, calm, and Tay. She closed her eyes and thought of how much she missed her best friend. She didn't think she'd ever loved anyone like she did Tay. She was Willow's whole everything and it felt like a piece of her was missing when they were on the road and Tay was thousands of miles away. She forced her eyes to shut as she wondered if everyone felt like that about their best friend.

Just as her mind began to relax, a queasy feeling rose in her as a familiar voice weaseled itself into her half-conscious. *You know what would be fun?* Willow jerked up with a startle and looked around to see who else might be up to distract her from herself. She shouted to her parents. "You okay hon? I'm taking the night shift. Dad's sleeping." Ror made eye contact with Willow through the rearview mirror while keeping focus on the road. "Yeah, fine. Just a bad dream I guess," her daughter responded quietly.

Willow walked back to J's calming area where he usually was doing self-soothing if she couldn't find him in his bunk above the captains' quarters (as her dad like to call the front seats).

J was barely rocking as he sat with his legs crossed and a blanket draped over his lap. Of course, he had his sunglasses on, and Blue was propped against the wall next to him. Those two spent a lot of time together, but sometimes everyone needs a break, even if it's from their favorite thing in the world.

He heard her enter his space and greeted Willow quietly, "Whoa." She sat on the ground about a foot from him and joined in his rhythmic rocking, knowing that it had an instant calming effect. She closed her eyes, and heard it again, *You know what would be fun?* Her eyes popped open like a set of broken blinds. J sensed the energy shift and Willow was worried he'd kick her out of his area. He'd never been afraid to tell any of them what he was thinking, and that on many occasions had been an unpopular opinion. Sometimes he was a dick about it too if Willow were honest. But she loved him, and she understood. That night, she needed him to be her soothing J, the platonic companion that is more a brother than an uncle. So, she told him outright.

"J, I'm having a bad night." He put his hand up for a fist bump, which she returned. He was in a good mood and Willow was grateful, especially since his show went longer than most and J had to be exhausted, too. Her heart jumped a little over the bond they shared and how lucky she was that he was in her life.

J may have had hundreds of thousands of fans that longed for his autograph or short interaction, but he was her family. Forever.

His response was soft and exactly what she was not so secretly hoping for. "Drops?" She smiled with exhaustion and just nodded her head yes. He scooted back to make room for Willow as she positioned herself beside his body and lay her head on the floor next to his leg. Rather than staring at the ceiling, she forced her eyes to close once again.

The voice was rushing in, and her body remembered it's power as the anxiety gathered in her gut. But this time the words she hated so much were crushed into stardust as a familiar sensation met the skin between her eyes. She could smell J's freshly washed hands as his middle finger padded in a steady rhythm she could not hear, but her soul knew like the lines of her own hands. Slow and soft, it was a technique they had used for years to help Willow sleep when her anxiety overwhelmed her. If he himself was in a good mental space, J always obliged.

He could tell when she calmed down, and when she fell asleep because her mom and dad would say that's always when he got up and put himself to bed. That night, it took some extra time and he hummed to himself as she pictured little droplets of water meeting her forehead. She could see rain and tried to smell it.

Finally, the sweetness was returning to her nose as she was interrupted by something strange.

She held her breath and waited. There it was again. She opened her eyes and J was staring at her with confusion. "Whoa? Baby go?" She realized he was right, that must have been the baby moving! She allowed her hands to float up to her swollen belly. The baby jumped again and she smiled. "He likes drops, J." His giggle was gentle and more for himself than anyone. "Baby like drops, J," he said to himself and continued gently tapping her forehead until all she could see was the darkness of night illuminated with stars cut from the sky above their home waiting patiently for them to return.

♥

It was finally *the* day. Willow and Ror were going through the final round of online families that were looking for a baby. Her heart felt all fluttery like it was mad and excited, and the baby hadn't kicked since the day before. She wondered if he was upset at her. Willow tried not to dwell on that thought as she sat at the table which moonlighted as her bed and laid her hands politely in her lap. She was acting weird, and her mom gave her the infamous raised eyebrow.

"Sorry, I'm just nervous, I guess. What if none of them are good enough? What if I can't find the right ones? What if..." Ror grabbed Willow's hand and put it up to her face. "What if there is someone that will love you both so much for this gift and that will give him a better life than you can offer him right now?" A smile came to her daughter's face as she grasped onto those words. *A better life.* Willow looked down at her little feet and ripped jeans and felt very fourteen. She nodded her head as a reassurance to herself but knew that her mom would take it in as well.

The little clicks of the laptop echoed throughout the bus as J slept and Max drove through Nevada toward home and some semblance of normalcy after tour. Willow saw her dad peek at them in the rearview mirror periodically and she stuck her tongue out and made silly faces at him.

He made a pig nose, broke into a smile, and said, "Love you, kid." His words always hit her deep and she couldn't help but display another big smile.

She couldn't pinpoint why or how, but the digital profiles staring at her through the screen seemed to amplify the urgency she'd already felt every time she flipped through the hard copy books that had so far held no solution to her search. The first page had what seemed like a billion families on it and every single one looked perfect. It seemed kind of gross, actually; how could they all possibly be so flawless? Doctors, chemists, even one lady that claimed to be a professional synchronized swimmer. Seriously, that one was ridiculous-who even does that kind of weird stuff? They were really over the top and like the others she'd already screened, most already had kids of their own. But it was the ones that didn't seem to be so sparkly and shiny that Willow found that she didn't trust. No one seemed good enough, but at the same time they were all too good to be true. She looked over at her mom and sighed.

"You doing okay kiddo?" She asked gently. Willow explained her dilemma and Ror gave her a squeeze. "I know hon. The reality is that no one will ever be quite good enough. This is your *child*. But when you find them, you'll know." Willow softly nodded and let herself melt into her mom as they scrolled a little bit more.

They tried starting in their home state of Oregon, but only one woman caught her eye and even she didn't feel quite right, although she was closer than most. Next, they used the filter to select some different options. Couples. Single parents. Gay. Mixed race. Conservative. Willow and Ror looked at them and they looked back, begging for a gift no one can ask for. Her heart felt heavy and very overwhelmed.

"I just need some time. I thought this would be the perfect way to pick them since the books didn't work, but somehow this is almost worse. I'll look through it with Tay later, I guess..." Willow explained to her parents as a gentle request for escape. Max looked back and winked at her from the mirror. "No problem, kid. Mom's right, you'll know when you see them. Don't give up. They're out there." She smiled and let them know she needed to lie down. It was only 8am, and by the time they got home they would be in a different time zone, so it was even earlier.

They told her to get some rest and Ror helped fold up the table and pull out Willow's bed. Then, she went up front to keep her husband company as she put on her Captain's hat and shut the partition behind her. "Ahoy cap'n, need a skipper this fine mornin'?" Max still thought she was hilarious after all those years together and Willow could hear their giggles sink into a light conversation.

She rolled her eyes as her head hit the pillow. *What dorks*, she thought. Her hand floated down to the spot on her belly it seemed to want to rest on lately and the baby kicked her softly. "I know, it is kind of cute. I promise, I'll find you some dorks of your own." And with the promise on her lips, she slipped away and dreamt once again of the night her biggest mistake became her greatest lesson in love.

When she awoke, Willow felt panicked. She stirred with an anxiety she hadn't ever known, which was the opposite of how she'd felt only moments before as she'd drifted so peacefully to sleep. But suddenly there was a drive she couldn't shake, a need to chronicle everything she was feeling-the baby, tour, her undeniably screwed up youth, and the strange beauty in all of it. Her heart raced with the thought that the life that grew within her would grow up without knowing the whole story... her story.

*What was I dreaming about?* She wondered to herself as she rummaged through the cubby above her bed. When her hands found it, Willow pulled out a spiderman notebook and a purple pen. Sitting down, her heart began to slow. As the pen touched the wide lined paper, she felt a stirring inside her womb.

"Wow, okay kid. I get it. I'm going, I'm going... stay tuned for your very own hot mess address."

She smiled, grateful that for some reason she was drawn to such an unexpected project. "I promise, it's not as bad as you probably think. How could it be, right? It ends with you, so it has the perfect ending no matter what," she said softly. And with that, she massaged her belly and began to write.

♥

*April 23, 2017*

*Well kid, I guess this is as good a place as any to start. A lot of life and pain and learning has happened between the day I found out about you and now. I have been driving myself and everyone else crazy going between pretending nothing was happening and completely melting down over what I would do with you, and for you. So, I decided to start doing this instead. Besides, it's not like I had a choice-you all but forced me to start this journal for you. I don't know if you ever would have let me fall asleep again if I hadn't. But I'm glad I gave in, because this is already pretty cool, and I like the idea that there will be something that's just between you and me.*

*I'm going to write to you because someday I want you to know what this experience was like from the start, or close to it, so that you will hopefully understand how we got to where we did. I know I lost a couple of months there, but it might be better that way since I am in a much less freaked out place than I was at first. It was some rough going there for a while! I got caught in a cycle of doctor's appointments, looking for your parents, and trying to be a kid. It mixed as well as it could, but it began to feel like groundhog's day there for a bit and I wish I could tell you how badly I just wanted to run away.*

*Not from my family, because they were about all that was holding me together. And not from Tay, because as always, she was incredible. It was more just reality that I wanted to escape. To just have a week, or even a day, when I was fourteen again and just me. Because with you, I will always feel worried, and scared, and hopelessly in love in a way that I'll never be able to undo again.*

*I love that, and at times I hate it too only for the fact that with that level of love comes the loss of my innocence. So instead, I wish for you to experience it fully. Be a kid, for the love of all that is good. Just let yourself enjoy doing every dumb, immature, and fun thing you want to while it's there. Be free. Don't do the things that all of us wish we hadn't, that always come down to trying to grow up too fast. I guess that's my first lesson to you as your mom. Let me loving you, creating you, be enough to inspire you to live the young life I won't get back. Want more for yourself and please use my choices as a lesson. I would never do any of it differently because now you have life and that will always be my greatest accomplishment.*

*I love you kid.*

*September 6, 2017*

*Today we're at seven months. Yes, I know, I skipped a LOT of time in there and I'm sorry bud. We got back from tour at the end of May, and we all tried to do the whole getting back to normal life thing. That was a little hard though, considering I was, you know, a pregnant kid and our little family was trying not to implode on a regular basis.*

*Dad and J spent a lot of time outside doing anything they could to stay busy. The summer was pretty well taken up with them repairing the whole fence, goat pens, barn, and basically anything else that would distract them from what was really happening. We decided as a family to postpone the last leg of the tour in Australia and Mom did some advanced damage control with the media and fans. She was able to provide full refunds to everyone and promised that J's next record would make the wait more than worth the while. And honestly, she couldn't be wrong because everything J puts out turns to gold, or platinum. As much as I was looking forward to visiting such an awesome place, by the time the conversation about it came around, I was out. My everything hurt, I was tired, heavy, and not in the mood for anything except being home.*

*Mom and I did have a killer garden this year and I helped her take care of it every morning and night. It did get to where weeding was out of the question so I had to surrender to watering and harvesting anything that was above ground or that I could get to on my hands and knees. Somewhere between July and August, my belly got so big I forgot what the bottom half of my body looked like. Mom had to help me shave my legs, which honestly, I'm still not that good at so I kind of was okay with. She also rubbed my feet a lot because they looked like little balloons by the time the sun set on most days.*

*I know, I'm just being gripey. I should have written to you before now, but I was kind of being selfish in spending my last summer as not a mom… or whatever I end up being to you. I spent a lot of afternoons on the porch rocking with Mom and Tay and going on walks around the property. What I did not do was spend time in town where anyone could see me. It was weird (and I hate to admit it, but embarrassing) to even think about someone outside of our family knowing my situation. I went to my doctor appointments in Boris and otherwise was home bound. It was my choice, but because we got this far and no one else is sure what's going on, it was worth it. I hope you can understand and forgive me for that.*

*Currently I feel like the cows I see all bloated in the pastures in spring. From the front I almost look normal at the right angle but from the side it looks like I stole a basketball and shoved it up my shirt. You are a cute bump, but you are not a small one by any means! The doctor says you're going to be a good-sized baby and by the way you tap-dance on my bladder and kick me in the ribs, I'd say you're definitely running out of space. Thank you for stopping your obsession with salsa and corn dogs and broccoli, but I wish you would have decided on liking any other candy than black licorice! It's okay though, I think I'm almost starting to like it so maybe you won this one. Anyway, here's to more of these little letters to you as we travel this crazy road together.*

*I love you already.*

*October 30, 2017*

*Well, I woke up about two hours ago completely confused. At first, I thought I had to poop. Like bad. It was like gas pain that doubles you over and feels like pressure at the same time. But now it's pretty clear what's going on... you are making your entrance into the world, and I am NOT ready for this yet!*

*I screamed out for Mom when I looked down and realized my pants were wet, too. We'd done the Lamaze classes and I knew we were clipping right along and honestly kid, it scared the hell out of me! My body was constricting in a way I have never dreamed would be possible. Like, a cat that got really scared and had its back arched to the sky. And my hips, they felt like they were rubber and it seemed like I was falling apart in every way. Oh, and it HURT-it hurt so bad kiddo. When it started, I had at least ten minutes between the misery sessions to catch my breath and completely panic. So, that was effective, obviously (not). Why wouldn't me crying and screaming help relax my body that was doing the same thing?*

*This entire experience is disgusting, no offense. In the fifteen minutes to the hospital, I did end up pooping uncontrollably twice. Yeah, I pooped my pants, son.*

*Okay, that's the only funny part now that I'm telling you about it, but at the time it was really gross and smelled worse than you probably think. I'll be level with you and admit that the first time I also puked. Mom wasn't sure what to do about that, so she just rubbed my back as Dad continued to drive furiously fast and gag over and over.*

*I still haven't gotten a shower but honestly, I can't care about that because I feel like I'm dying. Writing you is about the only thing I can do between contractions because it's something to focus on that isn't in this room that smells like sterile sheets that have been bleached too many times. Embarrassment is not something I have time for right now and I'm just so grateful my whole family is here to keep me from totally losing it. I do have a room of my own in the hospital and it's peaceful and calm, other than what my body is trying to do. It feels an awful lot like a storm ripping me open.*

*We are in Salt Lake City. J and Dad are waiting on the bus until we call them. Mom is in here with me. She's been resting her forehead against mine as I sit on the stupid exercise ball, breathing deep so I'll model her. When I cry, she cries.*

*We've taken a walk down the hall and back, and in the middle of it I had to lean into her because a contraction hit me so hard, I thought I would crumble.*

*I don't know how I'm going to get through this. My body seems so tiny and young compared to Mom's. I feel every bit of my fourteen years here, just too young for any of this. I think about Tay when my mind is clear enough, which isn't for more than a few moments at a time. I think of how the last time she and I talked she was planning to go to the mall and meet someone she had a crush on and-*

*Oh no, oh my god! I need to focus, kid. There's no more time between the pain. You are almost here, it's time. I'll see you on the other side of this.*

*I love you so much, I can't wait to meet you.*

*November 1, 2017*

Dad said that as soon as I saw you, I would forget everything that had to happen to bring you here. That was such a lie, but I appreciate his effort to make me feel better (as someone who hasn't been through giving birth himself).

Everyone was right, you really are a big boy! Almost nine pounds and a full head of hair, like your own dad. You have his nice skin tone, too. But when I look at you all I see is love. You are totally innocent, perfect, and unbroken. The second they laid you on my chest and our eyes met, I knew. You are my boy; you will always be. But I cannot be your mom.

They told me I labored for twenty hours before they sent a nurse to get the OR ready. The doctor let me try for too long, and I lost all strength. Because I had an epidural, I couldn't feel anything below my waist so I couldn't tell that nothing was changing, but I could feel that you were in trouble. I ended up needing a blood transfusion and an emergency C-section. I haven't really had time to think about how serious that was, but something deep inside me says that I am very lucky to be here to see you. That is so terrifying that I can't face it right now. Mom hasn't left my side yet, and it's been several hours.

She keeps kissing me and saying how proud she is of me, in a way that feels like she didn't expect this to be the outcome.

I still can't feel a lot of my body, which is a really yucky sensation. My legs just feel like chunks of meat I can't move like I should, but my arms work and I keep wanting to hold you but without being able to sit up, it's not safe. Currently, I have you tucked in next to me as I write this. Dad just got here and as soon as he saw you, he cried, and told me how much he loved me. He parked next to Mom in a chair and asked if they could hold you so I can nap.

Looking at you again, I can't believe that I made you. How is that possible? You and I are just kids in different stages, but we're bound forever. I don't know what your dad would think of you, but I can say he'd be wrong to think you are anything less than perfect. You are. Your nose is the cutest and your mouth is adorable. Ten fingers and toes, and that big noggin-they're all perfect. I want to keep looking at you forever, but I know you're hungry and that means it's bottle time.

The nurse is bringing one over that's already prepared so I'm going to let you suckle away until you pass out.

*My eyes are starting to get heavy too, so Dad is coming over to take you. I just kissed your hand as he lifted you up and took you to the rocker by Mom. As I see them watching over you, I am comforted knowing you are safe. I can't give you what you need, I'm not even comfortable enough with my own body to use it to feed you. But for now, you are safe, and you are loved. When I wake up, we will have to see what all of this means for both our futures.*

*November 2, 2017*

*Hey there kiddo. I just got up and it's 2pm. When I opened my eyes, I felt everything for the first time in days. The first thing I did was bolt up (which hurt really bad because of my stitches) and look for you. I panicked because I couldn't find you and jammed the call button as many times as I could until the nurses ran into the room. Already in tears, I begged to know where you were and they instantly apologized and said not to worry, that they had taken you to the nursery to rest while I did. I asked where my parents were, and the nurse said they'd gone out for lunch. Feeling less freaked out, I fell back on my pillow with a grunt.*

*Everything in my body aches and feels heavy, and the nurse said it's because of how long I labored. It feels like I ran for hours and hours and then cut my gut open. It's brutal. I still can't believe all of this is because I brought a person into the world, though. As much as I want to see you just to make sure you're breathing, I trust what the nurses said and that you need to rest uninterrupted. That said, I'm not going to leave you alone for long. In the meantime, there's one person I HAVE to talk to. Mostly so you can get a front seat perspective of how we work, I'll let you in on the conversation as best I can.*

*As the phone rings I'm tearing up just waiting to hear her voice. She answers and I break out into sobs.*

*"Hello?" I'm trying to suck up the snot and choke back the tears to say it back, but I can't. Her voice is worried as she repeats herself. "Hello? Willow is that you? Ror? Oh god, is she okay?" I realize the alarm I'm causing and force myself to squeak some real words out. "Tay! It's me." She's relieved, I can tell, and she starts crying just because I am. "What's wrong? Is the baby okay? How are you?" I remember I don't have too long probably before you, Mom and Dad are back, and I can't stop thinking about your cute little face so I give her a quick rundown of what I can remember.*

*She adds, "Oh my gosh, Will. I'm so glad it's over! I can't believe you're someone's mom." I tell her I know, me either, but I don't know that I really am, which of course is returned by questions from her. "Tay, I don't know what to do. He's perfect, like this little angel. But legit, we're in middle school, girl. I've only had my period for two years and am still embarrassed to talk about it. Do you know how gross it is to have people talking to me about how to use my boobs to feed him? I can't do it; I'm using bottles already-it seems creepy or something not to. I don't know."*

"And I can't even get a job for two years, how am I supposed to take care of him? He deserves parents-real, adult parents. I'm just not that. And I couldn't settle on a family from any of the adoption sites or books, so he doesn't have a family to go home to, either. I don't know what to do Tay!"

I'm starting to freak out again and then realize that I've been so selfish not even asking her how it went with her crush Luis. "By the way, how was the mall date? Does Luis like you back?" She sighed and said what we both were feeling, "Yeah, I think so, but that seems kind of small compared to all this, Will. We'll talk about it later." She can tell I'm tired by the way I'm starting to fade so we say goodbye and I make sure to tell her that I love her. "Love you too. I know everything is scary right now, but it's going to be okay. I'm so proud of you."

As I hang up my phone, I take a quick picture of my stitches and send it to her so she can see how gnarly it is. I lay back and look at the ceiling for a few minutes until I hear the sweetest sound that pulls my heart back to full consciousness, even though I'm exhausted. You're crying and I can tell you're hungry again, so I reach out to take you from the nurse. I ask for a bottle, cuddle you close to me and watch you eat.

*The way Mom rushes in the room when she realizes I'm awake and you're with me, I can tell that she wanted to be back before I woke up. Dad isn't with her, and she said he went on a walk with J to burn some energy. I'm a little relieved that she and I are alone because I want some time to talk with her about you. We walked into this room with the understanding that we would be calling your new parents when you arrived, and we would be leaving without you. But I never was able to choose anyone good enough for you so I can't do that now and I need to tell her.*

*She comes over and kisses my forehead and strokes your cheek. Her eyebrows wrinkle as she looks at me and asks how I'm feeling. I tell her about how I don't have any energy and I think about how they told me some of the details of your birth and I ask her what I already know, but I need to hear someone say it. "Mom, did I almost die?" Her eyes well up and I can see her considering if she can lie about this to protect me, but she must have decided against it.*

*She tells me with a worried tone, "Yeah baby. You did. We almost lost you, that's why you had the transfusion and they had to take him c-section. Your body wasn't made for this yet."*

She shakes as she looks at me and asks again how I feel today. I tell her that, like I already said, I'm too tired and everything makes me want to sleep. She asks if I've been bleeding and I tell her that honestly, I have no idea. She gets a worried look on her face and lifts my blanket quickly and looks. I pull it back down and frown, embarrassed. "Mom!"

She touches my foot gently and puts her head on the edge of the bed in relief. "Sorry hon didn't mean to embarrass you. Thank God, you're not bleeding. If you do, push your call button immediately!" I'm starting to get scared, and you can feel it so you start to cry. I ask her what's going on and she explains about hemorrhaging, and how that is what happened yesterday and how dangerous it can be. Apparently, the risk decreases after a few days but until then we are hanging out in the hospital.

Before she sits down, she scoops you up and cradles you, so you are calm again. I'm relieved to let her take you because I want to drink some water and talk about the important thing that's hanging over us. I grab the bulky cup with the ugly fat bendy straw the hospital gave me and suck it down in almost one swallow. I also realize that my lips are dry and that Mom left me some Dr. Pepper lip balm on my tray and put some of that on.

*She looks at me, knowing I want to chat. I try to adjust to face her, but my stomach sends a shock that tells me that it's a little too soon to try that yet, so I just turn my head toward her.*

*"What's up, hon?" She says and waits as I pull my eyes away from you and how naturally you lie in her arms. I figure there's no use in doing anything but being direct, plus I feel like a truck hit me, and I'm fading fast. "Mom, obviously I can't keep him. Kids aren't meant to raise kids, at least I'm not. But I can't give him up. I can't watch someone walk out the door with him and know he's theirs now. I can't trust anyone to take care of him!" I'm obviously crying again because I guess that's what I do now. She starts rocking the chair and you let out the sweetest coo. She looks down at you and is silent until my tears slow down and I'm calmer. I know she's not ignoring me; she's always been so good about letting me feel things completely and not shaming me for whatever it is.*

*Mom looks back at me and says quietly, "Kiddo, I get it. And I knew this would be an impossible choice for you. I know you wanted to pick out a family for him, but I feel the same way. This is a forever thing. Dad and I were talking at lunch and… God how do I even say this to you?"*

*My eyes get huge as I wonder what she could be afraid to say to me. "What? What Mom?" I don't have patience normally, but right now especially. She replies unsteadily, "Will, what if Dad and I raise him, and when you think he's old enough you can tell him that you're his birth Mom? People have done this since forever and I'd rather make sure we give him what he needs. I'm sorry, you cannot raise him yourself, Dad and I both agreed that's not an option-and we know that you understand that you're just not ready. What... what do you think?" I swear I see a bead of sweat fall down the side of her face.*

*I nod my head gently as I stare at you and once again wonder how I could have made and birthed you-almost died to give you life-and yet we all agree I'm nowhere near equipped to be your mom. I think about you taking your first steps and saying your first word and how badly I want to be there for that. At the same time, I realize those things may be happening before I'm even able to drive.*

*I look at Mom, the most loving, kind, and fitting parent I could imagine having other than Dad, who is a gentle discipliner and an unwavering support. In this moment I realize how perfect they are and how lucky I am to have them. No one gets to choose their parents, but I do get to pick yours.*

*It hits me what an opportunity this is and that the best choice for you is to give you the best I know of. I smile at Mom and then to you.*

*"Thank you, Mom. Thank you so much. Do you mean it? You guys will keep him?" She laughs at my wording. "He's not a puppy, hon. But yes, he's part of us and it breaks my heart to think of doing anything but keeping it that way. Dad, too. We're definitely not young this time around but I think we have one more go round in us." She winks at me and adjusts your bottle. "By the way, Will. He still needs a name. Do you have any in mind?"*

*I hadn't let myself think of names because I thought your parents should decide what fit you best. But since I laid eyes on you, one name has been stuck in my head like it already belonged to you. "Elijah," I tell her. I pause and think about what would have great meaning to our family, and to you as a person and realize there's only one middle name you could have. "Elijah Jordan Ellingson."*

*She looks back at me with so much warmth I can almost feel it. "It's perfect, Will." I ask her to bring you to me for a second and I kiss you on the cheek which makes you squirm and coo at me. "I'm going to take a nap, guys. I love you, Mom. Love you, Lij."*

*The nickname comes out of my mouth as if I've said it a thousand times before and as I drift off to sleep, I think about how grateful I am that we don't have to say goodbye after all.*

*November 10, 2017*

*Your first week at home has been rough, bud. Not only have I not mentally prepared myself for having a baby come home with me, I also didn't expect to have the jealousy that I've been hit with. Every time you cry, I run to get to you and find Mom or Dad is already there. I know it's what we've agreed to, and it's what's best for all of us, but man it's harder than I ever could have expected. Watching you grow up is going to be such a gift but it's also going to hurt knowing that I need to keep a little distance for it to be healthy. Hoping that gets better with time as our family kind of shuffles itself into this new thing we've become. Until then, we're just being careful with one another because I think we're all a little fragile.*

*My moods are all messed up still and everything continues to make me cry, which is so annoying. At least a lot of the time it's happy tears now. J made mac and cheese for dinner, and I started bawling as I poured ketchup on it and ate happily. Wow, I just realized this is the first time since you were born that I've really talked about him, which is weird. He's such a huge part of your world. He and Dad had talked about you joining the family and Dad said that J screeched and jumped up and down because he was so excited.*

*I've been the only kid J's ever really been around, except Tay and her sister of course, but he acts like it's the most natural thing in the world to him that you are here. The other day when I finally got to take a shower, you had been taking a nap and I heard you crying. I rushed out in my towel to make sure you were okay and saw J sit down in the chair with you and start rocking away. He hummed his one tone note to you and I ran back to the bathroom because it was gross that he had seen me in my towel (although really, I don't know if he noticed me since he had his eyes shut as he rocked). That motion is something J really needs to be soothed and I know you need it to. I have a feeling you two will be spending lots of time in the rocker together. Just wait until he plays Blue for you, that's something that will change your world, kid.*

*I did help Mom give you a bath today. You looked so peaceful when we poured the warm trickle of water down the back of your head. She showed me how to take care of your belly button (which is harder than it sounds) and how to wash a little boy. You were squirmy and slippery, so it was good that I had another set of hands. After we dried you off, Mom let me put lotion and baby powder on you and get you dressed in your diaper and jammies. I was surprised how relaxing that whole thing ended up being for me.*

*You were sleepy and that helped, but the smell of you with the lotion on your new skin made me feel really at peace for some reason.*

*I just gave you a bottle and put you to bed for the night. I think I'm going to see if Tay wants to come meet you tomorrow since we have to start thinking about what we want to do for the talent show. I'm hoping we can do a lip-syncing routine that is silly so we have fun and people aren't bored. We'll see, we might just decide to sit in the crowd and watch everyone else embarrass themselves instead of us.*

*We also need to catch up on some gossip because Tay and Luis dated for like three weeks and then he cheated on her. I feel bad for her, but all I can think about is how far from me I want guys to be for a while. I love you, so much. But you are a reminder of the choices I've made as well, and what we've been through is something I'll never forget as long as I live. I don't regret you-don't you ever think I would. I'm so glad to add you to our family, but I think with time I will really be sad that it wasn't in a different part of my life, so you could be mine. Really mine. But it needs to be like this, and Mom and Dad are so obsessed with you, it makes me smile right now just thinking of how excited they are to have you here.*

*I'll tell you a little secret that they won't: they always wanted more kids. Mom didn't think she could have babies as it was, then along came me. But they tried for a while after me to have another and it just never happened. You were meant to be, exactly as you are.*

*I've been thinking today about what you'll think of me when you're old enough to know. Will you be mad? Embarrassed? Ashamed? I hope not. We will always refer to you as my brother because that's how you'll be raised. But I think in your heart that even before you are told, you'll know that you and I are one.*

*I love you, Lij. I'm going to go call Tay real quick, but I'll see you in the morning.*

*November 11, 2017*

*Well, as expected, you are obsessed with Tay. You couldn't take your eyes off her and I swear I saw you smile like a hundred times when she talked to you. She just left and I put away the pizza box and pop cans before I put you in your wiggly chair that makes you gurgle and laugh. Right now, you're looking at the little mobile of stars over your head like they're the most surprising thing you've ever seen. You're such a stinking cutie!*

*Tay and I caught up about the whole Luis situation and how he made out with Katie R., which she recorded on her phone and sent to Tay. Super brutal. Tay made a big deal out of dumping him on social media and texted him and said if he ever said anything bad about her, she was going to send the video to his parents (because his mom is her hairdresser, so she has her number). Anyway, it seems to have settled that mess. So much drama! I liked soaking it in though, because it feels like forever since I've done or even heard of anything to do with anyone my age.*

*I was terrified to ask her, but I had to see if the other people in our grade knew about you. Don't get me wrong, I am NOT ashamed of you at all.*

*I am ashamed of myself for the night of choices I made that led to you being here, and I'd just rather that no one know about it. No one (especially Mom and Dad) knows that it wasn't all my choice and it almost got so much worse before I got away. It's just not something I like to think about, and I am so scared of people mocking me if they ever find out.*

*Anyway, I was shocked when she got these huge eyes, took a bite of pizza, and smiled at me. She said, "Dude, I don't think anyone has a clue. You've been on the road with J most the year and even when you were home you weren't showing. Guess it won't seem that weird that in the same period, your mom had a baby." She shrugged and then looked at you before sticking out her tongue and making a funny face. It made you smile and your eyes light up.*

*I wish I could say I wasn't relieved to hear her say that, but I really was. Lij, I have always been such a good kid. I've done some dumb things before, like stealing some nail polish and little stuff that was stupid. But I've never been the kind of girl that does, that. I'm so afraid people will call me a slut, or a whore. None of that is your fault, it has nothing to do with you. I'm just coming to grips with the fact that I have done things that I never saw myself doing.*

*I wasn't raised that way and I don't know what got into me. Maybe I'm not as good of a girl as I thought. I don't know, bud. This feels weird to be telling you of all people, but I also really want to be sure you have the entire story from the beginning. Nothing hidden, no questions to answer. I promise I won't give you this info until I think you're ready, and that won't be for a long time.*

*For now, I'm going to see about doing the exercises the doctor showed me to strengthen my stomach muscles again. You seem tickled where you are, so I'll let you play with the stars to your heart's content.*

*December 15, 2017*

OMG Lij, I just got home from the end of year dance! Tay and I had so much fun, but the guys were lame. They all stayed on one side of the gym, and we were on the other. I wonder if they were talking about how to ask us to dance, because none of them made a move until the night was almost over. It was painfully awkward, let's just say that.

There were a few times I saw Alex and Erica whispering and looking over at me. I don't think they know about you, but what if they do? I know, that's not the kind of thing that maybe I should say to you. I'm not ashamed of you, bud. I'm ashamed of me. I know, I JUST said that last time I wrote you, and I'll tell you that in these letters a million times but it's important for you to know. Plus look at me, I'm gushing over middle school boys while you're doing tummy time and being super mad you got some shots today. For the record, I'm rubbing your back and singing to you in between sips of pop and blurbs of writing. I want to make you feel better, but I am selfishly so grateful I didn't have to stay home and take care of you tonight. Please don't hate me for that.

My body is sucking back into shape, except my boobs which just insist on being huge.

*A lot of girls wouldn't complain about that, but it makes it hard for me to fly under the radar when I stick out from everyone else. Mom let me have some of her old sports bras to hide them a little though, so that should help. Before I met your dad, I was always trying to get the attention of guys. After you, I don't really care for them to look at me. It's not the same now, knowing what happens beyond innocent flirting. It's too much, way too much and I don't want anything to do with that again for a LONG time.*

*Anyway, I did get my first slow dance tonight. It was with James, who I've never thought of as anything more than a friend. He and Tay had a crush on each other for a while but she's way over that and was pushing me to talk to him. He's kind of nerdy but super funny! When he put his arms on my waist, I put mine on his shoulders and we didn't look at each other for the whole song, but it felt special anyway, like I mattered to him in the kind of way that makes a memory you have forever. I hope I was his first dance too, because as dorky as that is, it would still be cute.*

*Tay didn't dance with any guys since she's still mad about Luis, but we had the most fun jamming to every fast song that came on. She asked the DJ to play our song and when he did, we remembered the dance we made up last year and busted it out in front of everyone.*

*Honestly, it didn't even embarrass me because she was there with me. When I'm with Tay, I feel like the rest of the world doesn't exist. I love her and I love being around her. In fact, for a while I thought I liked her. You know, like liked her. But after giving myself a lot of time to think about it, I realized that it's easy to confuse friendship and a relationship when you're my age. That might be the most grown-up thing I've said that isn't related to you!*

*I've seen how my moods and feelings can shift with the wind, so it doesn't surprise me too much that the one person that has seen me through everything is someone I thought I might have feelings for. One night I even tried to kiss her! I know, it's a little weird to tell you that, but someday you'll be fourteen or fifteen and you'll be confused about everything in your world and I just want you to know that whatever ends up being the truth in your life, it's normal to not have a clue what that is while you're still transforming every single day. For the record, when I leaned in and closed my eyes, Tay bust out laughing. The only spit I got on me was from her spraying it everywhere as she cracked up.*

*I looked at her eyes and felt love, but in the way that she was the other half of my heart-my family, my best friend, but not my girlfriend.*

*She was right, but I'm glad that now I know for sure. I just shook my head and said definitively, "Yeah, no. Never mind!" We got up, did our secret handshake, and went to the kitchen and made burritos to eat as we did our homework. There was no shame or mocking, we carried on as if everything was okay, because it was. I hope that's the kind of real and honest friendship everyone has with their best friend because it's sad to think they don't.*

*December 8, 2018*

*Sorry I missed so much time again, bud! The last year was jam packed with everything that makes being home amazing. Seeing you look at snow for the first time and wiggle around as you gazed at Christmas lights made winter pretty awesome. Jumping in puddles, playing softball (which I am NOT good at), and staying in and watching movies stole springtime. And swimming, junk food, sleep overs, camping, and making s'mores in the backyard took up the summer, which was a welcome return after it being such a different thing last year while we waited for you to get here. It was incredible and I wouldn't have changed a single minute of any of it. Having you now makes every second our family lives such a richer experience, it's like we get to do it all over again through you and your fresh joy and wonder.*

*School started up again in September of course and it is going great so far. I get to go in person again, and it has been awesome getting to just enjoy being a normal student. I get to sit in class all day and be bored, write notes that I pass to Tay when I can, and come home to you and see how much you have changed since I left in the morning. I swear that there isn't a day that you stay the same anymore.*

*You are growing, learning, and becoming your own little person more with every day that passes. I insisted that we take you trick or treating for Halloween, and you were the absolute cutest little scarecrow anyone has ever seen, I'm positive. You weren't a fan of the face paint and had it wiped all over everything before the night was over, but we got to show you off and that was fun, even if everyone was congratulating Mom and Dad instead of me. When we got home, we had your first birthday, and it was so fun to watch you try to blow out your little candle and smash cake all over your highchair tray. We took a million pictures of it, I taped one to the back of this entry for you. I gave you a stuffed monkey as your present and you've been pretty much glued to it since the moment you got it and that makes me feel pretty special.*

*Thanksgiving was good, but nothing really to write home about. Grandma Char made a yummy dinner, and we all went over and ate until we could hardly move. You mowed down on the sweet potatoes, like you were OBSESSED with them, and I couldn't help but laugh when you slapped your tray and said, "Mmmm!" every time Mom gave you a bite.*

And that brings us up to date. It's Christmas and we did such a cheesy family portrait, but it was also kind of badass. J was so excited to wear tights because of the compression. He's been wearing them since he woke up, and we didn't even take the pictures until three. I know, he makes me laugh too-such a goofball. He made a pretty rockin' elf with his shades and of course we caught an action shot of him dancing. I tried to look like a hippie with no makeup and a long wig that I put a couple little braids in, and a peace sign in one hand and a candy cane in the other. Mom laughed so hard at all this and called me her mini me, which I secretly liked a lot because she's gorgeous, you know?

Anyway, she and Dad were the coolest looking Santa and Mrs. Claus I've ever seen, with his long curly dark hair to go with the fake beard and Mom looking like Janis Joplin in her short red dress with white trim and awesome platform shoes. She sat on his lap and held you, with your tiny little Santa hat and costume. We were all so happy that you were awake and only cried once, when J farted so loud it made everyone laugh and startled you into a frenzy. I included pictures of that too because they're hilarious.

*Now that all the excitement is over, you're chilling out in your walker, which is extra cute since you're still in your red onesie and the black socks that look like boots. I just kissed the top of your head and you looked up at me and for once, it was like looking in my own eyes. You are really starting to look like me, which is fun.*

*I must admit that I still get stabs of jealousy sometimes when it comes to you. I even had a heated conversation with Dad about your bedtime the other day. I wanted you to stay up twenty minutes so I could play with you when I got home from Tay's, but he had already put you to bed. I actually yelled at him and said he was trying to keep you from me. I told him it was bullshit, and you were still my kid. Being Dad, he pulled me close to him and hugged me and laid his head on the top of mine and said, "He'll always be your son, but you chose us to be his parents, kiddo. Please trust us." It made me cry; I couldn't help it. Sometimes the part of me that's your mother is so strong and I want to do all the things that prove that I am guiding you through life. But then I remember that I don't even know how to do that for myself and take a step back.*

*This choice I made for you is the right one, absolutely.*

*But it comes with some harsh sacrifices that really hurt sometimes. None of that matters though if you're taken care of the way you deserve.*

*Love you, Lij.*

*December 30, 2018*

*Well, today was the day, kid. You're at the table eating some food that Mom and I made, waving your arms as you sit in your highchair, shaking your head and spitting it out. Oh no! You just spit it at Mom and J is dying of laughter. Haha, Dad just asked him to do circles in the other room because you started spitting more and laughing after J did. What a circus!*

*We all just got back from the courthouse where we filed the paperwork naming Mom and Dad as your parents. It's official, I'm your sister, I guess. And technically your mom, too... that sounds super gross. I guess we'll just look at me as your sister from now on, but when you're old enough, we can talk about the mom stuff. I honestly don't know why we waited this long, other than maybe I wasn't quite ready to take the step until now. But it feels right, and it's almost a new year. What better way to start it than by giving everyone a fresh beginning?*

*The one person who has been missing from all of this is probably the one you want to know about, and that's your birth dad. I wish I could give that to you. I wish I knew anything at all about him, but I just don't. Believe me, I have looked up everyone with his first name (as I remember it) in the country on social media–I swear.*

*I'll keep looking though because you deserve to know both sides of the life that created you. Plus, I'd like to know what kind of people you come from, other than me. I have a lot of protection in my heart over you this way. I may be young, but I know how important it is to know your roots.*

*I'm about to start social studies homework because Mrs. Peters hates our class and gave us assignments during winter break. Before I do my reading, I just wanted to be sure to make a special letter about today. I included a copy of the paperwork, in case you wanted to see it, and your birth certificate so you don't think I'm crazy and making up the other part, although the letters before now should be pretty good proof.*

*Love you, kid.*

*January 3, 2019*

Well, Mr. Cranky pants, you are in full teething mode! It's both heartbreaking and irritating to hear you crying so often from the pain of your little teefers coming in. You have a bunch that have already broken through, and you are munching on everything you can get your hands on, which thankfully has only been stuff you're supposed to have so far. Except J's finger, that was an oopsie that made him howl. Of course, when he screamed it made you cry and the whole mess continued until I picked you up and was able to rock you while we listened to some music. Once you were calm you slapped me in the face because you were still upset, and I put you in the crib and told Mom (who was in the bathroom getting ready) that I needed to go. I'm not sure if I'm proud of that moment or not, but I figured it was better than you seeing me mad. It's funny how something as small as your tiny hand can shatter my heart so quickly.

I'm taking a walk while I wait for the tears to dry and my feelings to get smaller. I think about volleyball tryouts that are tomorrow and how much I hope that I'm in good enough shape to make the club team. It would mean a lot of weekend games and the thought of being home long enough to play a whole season makes me smile.

*I've never not been on the road for this long of a stretch and it is hard to describe what it's like to finally grow some roots. Part of me is hesitant and figures that tour will be here sooner than I know it, but the other part is curious where this could lead. Maybe Tay and I will hang out with more of the girls in our class that aren't total jerks. Or, maybe we'll just get to have more adventures than we've gotten to have in a long time. It feels good to know that my life is returning to normal. As I look down and see the giant rack that still insists on sticking around, I remember that I'll never quite be the same as I was last year. But I wouldn't have it any other way because even if you are a mean little turkey right now, I never want to go a day without squishing your sweet little cheeks and kissing your perfect face. We're all where we need to be right now and I'm grateful. I take a deep breath of the fresh chilly air and let it fill me with the hope of new beginnings.*

*I'll see you in a little bit, kid. I love you.*

*January 7, 2019*

*Hey little dude! Guess what? I made the team. And not just any-I get to play on the A team! I was so nervous at tryouts and even missed most of my serves. But Coach Rich said she was impressed with my setting and that I have a lot of potential. So, yeah, I guess that happened! And yes, of course Tay tried out too. She made the B team which is still cool because we will get to practice together and have games on the same days. It does suck a little because we won't get to play in games together, obviously. I'm just proud of us for making it because a lot of girls tried out and only twelve made it on each team. So yeah, I'm stoked bud!*

*Mom and Dad took all of us out for ice cream to celebrate tonight. It was fun and relaxing, and I think we all really enjoyed it. The only weird thing that happened was that for the first time since we've been home, J had a fan interrupt us to meet him. He usually matches the over excited energy which is why we avoid him meeting fans (if possible) since it's hard to get him calmed back down once he has a panic attack. But tonight was, like I said, just different.*

*This lady came up to our table saying she loved J's music and was so happy to meet him.*

She didn't shake his hand or try to look in his eyes like a lot of people do, which Mom and Dad noticed (I could tell because they were looking at the woman intently, Mom's eyes squinting in focus). J acknowledged her passively and said thanks. But, the lady said, she had someone that was an even bigger fan and really wanted to meet him.

It was at that moment we all realized there had been a short, small woman standing behind her the whole time. She was so shy and giggling lightly, waving at J, and saying under her breath "Wow it's Jordan Blue, wow he's here…" To all our surprise, he got up, grabbed the shy woman's hand, and started doing his rocks with her as he closed his eyes and shook his head. He pointed to himself and introduced to her, "Jordan." She squealed and continued to rock with him as she pointed at her own chest with an open palm and stated, "Amelia." We all just sat there with our mouths agape.

Lij, J doesn't do that. He doesn't like to meet new people unexpectedly and he doesn't go out of his way to dance with them in a Dairy Queen on a random Wednesday night in front of God and everyone. It was bizarre!

*Anyway, Amelia's mom left their phone numbers and said if J and Amelia wanted to get together again, he was welcome to call. J dramatically replied, "Yes please, again!" She looked back as she walked away and smiled and shook her head, a gesture that Mom returned. The women were bonded by having family that was different and unpredictable, an experience that had brought them both pain and heartache. But sometimes on a perfect night, those people they love that live differently will gift everyone with the experience of true joy in motion.*

*I'm not sure what Amelia's disability is, I think Down's Syndrome? But she is adorable! She's got amazing style, and her blonde hair was perfectly smooth like a calm lake. Her smile is infectious and even though they're strangers she made J so, so happy! I don't know if they'll ever see each other again (although I'd say there's a good chance) but that was a highpoint of an already pretty great day.*

*And now I get to read to you as you sit on my lap in your fuzzy footy pajamas. I may have school in the morning but for now, I'm all yours and you're mine. Mom and Dad will be in to kiss you goodnight soon and until then I'm going to read to you about Goodnight Moon.*

*January 14, 2019*

*Lij, today something big happened. I don't even know how to tell you this without breaking out in goosebumps, but... I found your dad.*

*I am a big mix of every kind of emotion, but the one that stomps them all is anger. I'll get to why that is in a while. Before that, I want you to know all the good things I found out about him because there is always a little good in everything and everyone.*

*To start with, his name is Brick Montgomery. Yeah, Brick, I know. He goes by his middle name though, which is Aaron. Guess I can't really blame him there. He is older than I figured he'd be. The night we met I got the impression he was a couple of years older than me, but it sounds like he's more like three, which makes him almost eighteen. His family is rich. There's no better way to say it than that, kid. His Dad, which technically is your grandfather, is a Senator in Georgia and his mom is just beautiful. I don't know what she does for a living, but I hope she's something brilliant like an engineer or a biologist or something. Either way, it's safe to say you come from good stock with all the superficial stuff like looks and brains and money. It's no wonder you're so handsome, bud.*

*You may have my eyes, but you have his perfect nose and cunning little half smile.*

*You have to be wondering how I know all of this, right? Well, that is where I wish I could just stop, so that what you know is neutral (and even good for the most part) and so you would never think negative of him. But that wouldn't be the truth, my sweet boy. I don't want to tell you, but I've come this far in being completely honest with you and I refuse to change that just because we've reached the tough stuff. So, hang on and know that what you're about to read does not reflect on you-not now, not ever. If you're not ready right now, save it for when you are because it's okay to take your time since there are some things you can't unknow once you've been told them.*

*This morning while I was eating my cereal, Dad was feeding you little chunks of bananas and pears. You were mushing it all into a sticky pile and laughing your face off about it. That laugh is like sunshine, and it was impossible for us not to giggle at you, until you smashed it into your hair and flung it on the walls. Mom face palmed and finished the sandwich she'd made for my lunch, tossed it in the bag, and carried you off for a bath. Dad and I were still laughing as he cleaned up, even though you were being naughty.*

*Sometimes that's when you're the very cutest though, when you're doing something you know you're not supposed to and think it's funny.*

*Anyway, the TV was on, and I was watching the news because that's what Dad has on in the mornings. There was a story on about a court hearing that was starting today. As the news writers wanted me to, I hung on until after the commercial to see the details. Mom heard it and yelled to Dad from the bathroom to turn it up. "That's that monster from over there in Georgia-right? Did they ever find that little girl?" She poked her head out as she held you in her arms, all wrapped up in your towel with rubber duckies on it.*

*Dad pointed at the TV, completely glued to it. "I don't know but that kid should never see the light of day again." I haven't ever heard Mom and Dad talk like that about anyone. If they have something bad to say about someone, at least they have good enough judgment to talk about it behind closed doors, which I've heard a time or two about people that have pissed them off-especially when it comes to one of us or J. But this was different, they were on fire with rage, and I had no clue what they were talking about. So, I asked.*

"That kid right there, he raped a girl in his hometown and he... he just hurt her really bad. But because his dad is the Senator, he couldn't afford to get caught, too high profile. She told her parents and the following day, she was gone. Vanished while they were asleep. They still haven't found her, at least not that I've heard." I asked him how old she was, and what her name was. "Thirteen. Jessica...Morris, I think it is." My stomach felt gross and sad, and a lot of different things as I imagined such a scary thing happening to someone my age. I looked at you and then I looked back at the TV which zoomed in on a young guy in a nice suit. With hair that he combed back with his fingers, skin that was slightly tinted olive and a smile that was handsome and clever. My heart dropped into my stomach.

Suddenly a rush of information connected, and I felt like I would fall over. The money, the politician father, the kind of people that run in smart circles and have more money than God but no one to answer to when they mess other people's lives up. The words that haunted me for over a year screamed in my head. YOU KNOW WHAT WOULD BE FUN? It was, without any doubt, him.

I have no idea what my reaction looked like obviously, but it must have been dramatic because Dad looked at me with huge eyes and asked me, "Willow? What's wrong?"

*"Are you okay?" He rushed over and gave me a hug. "I know kiddo, it's awful and he's such a huge asshole. They'll find her. They will. It's okay, kid." It wasn't until he stepped back that I realized I was absolutely sobbing. I looked at you again, and then at him, tracing the lines that I wished more than anything that I could deny. But they were set in stone. You are his, Lij, and I am so, so sorry that I couldn't give you better. I looked at Dad and couldn't speak yet, but I pointed at the screen, reading his name for the first time accurately. Brick Aaron Montgomery. Then, I pointed at you and lost what was left of the composure I was holding onto.*

*Mom had rushed in by then and was as concerned and confused as Dad. She was bouncing you on her hip and following my finger and tears. And then it hit her too, like a.... Brick. She gasped, piecing together what it all meant. "Oh no baby, is he really? Is that him?" I felt like I was in a different place, detached, like nothing was real suddenly, but I do remember nodding and sitting back down.*

*Dad couldn't look at us. He just kept repeating, "Holy shit. Holy shit," as it seemed like he realized that he easily could have been viewing my picture on the screen, along with pleas for information of my whereabouts.*

*That it could have been me in her shoes, that was missing, that had been hurt, that had been raped and maybe killed. It was almost me.*

*I honestly cannot think much more about any of this right now, and I don't think it's good to dwell on in this letter to you. It is important that you know who your biological father is, even though I hate how stuffy that term is. But it's true, he may have helped make you but he's not the one raising you. He won't be the man that helps shape who you become. His mistakes do not have to define who you are, Lij-never forget that. You have parents that live to see you succeed. You have me in your corner every step of the way. J will be your greatest ally every day of your life, and truly your biggest fan. Trust me, I understand how unfair this is to you and I want more than anything in this world to take this truth away from you but if I didn't tell you now, it would always be the missing piece that you needed to be whole. And there are people in this world who never find what that piece is. I don't want to see you go through that, so even if you have moments where you hate me for telling you all this, or for it being true, I hope you can one day be grateful that you never had to wonder.*

*I don't know what they will decide in this case, but I hope that they find Jessica and I really hope she is alive.*

*I feel a special kinship with her, another kid that deserves to be having cereal with her family this morning and laughing around the dinner table with them tonight.
Her bed is unslept in, and her parents have to be worried beyond description. I look at you and cannot bring myself to consider what it must be like in their shoes, not knowing.*

*Your father did this, and the truth will come out. But it is not your fault, and it never will be. You are living, breathing proof that even monsters have a piece of them that is untainted and pure. Like I said before, everyone has a little good in them and looking at his face as he smiles and refuses to answer the judge's questions, I shiver and realize that the best part of him is no longer his at all. You are ours, and Mom, Dad, J, and I will spend the rest of our lives proving to you that you are the greatest thing that ever could have happened to us.*

*I love you so much Lij and I hope someday you will find peace in me telling you this. Right now, it seems like a giant and terrifying nightmare. Instead of letting myself think of it more, I'm going to pick you up and we're going to dance in the living room until you fall asleep. Tonight, I need to be able to tuck you in and watch your little chest rise and fall in the soft light of your room.*

*Then, maybe I can lay my head on my pillow and try to find peace in knowing that in this moment, we can protect you from this world that I have brought you into. It may not be much but right now is all we have and all that we are ever promised.*

*God, I love you Lij. Please know that you are the breath that will always give me life.*

Months passed and life moved on at a particularly unfair pace for those who wished it to be in slow motion. Spring blossoms bloomed, wilted, fell, and shriveled in what felt like hours. The Ellingsons had made one decision that affected everyone in their world in a big way.

At Jordan's request, Max and Ror had agreed to take a hiatus on touring. After all they had been through since Willow found out she was pregnant, they had to admit that a break was just what the doctor ordered. In fact, they agreed to see what felt right for the rest of Jordan's career as a musician, because even he stated with a puff, "So tired..." And that had summed it up.

After more than a decade of world tours and seven full length albums, he was ready to step back and enjoy Blue within the confines of the farmhouse where they all lived. He was beginning to crave the magical silence the farm had brought with it, and he was ready to resume his duties on the property which from the beginning had created their own kind of satisfaction and peace. Plus, he had a new woman in his life to entertain and with that came the usual sacrifices required to make space for someone else.

Ror called the neighbor kid, Dean, that they had always hired to look after the animals when they were away.

She offered to pay him out for the rest of the month so he wouldn't be short on his bills and promised to call whenever they left town again. After that, the property was back in their hands and Ror too, was relieved to be home for good.

Willow and Taylor enjoyed their first season of club volleyball and the pride and defeat that comes with competing with their peers. For them, it was a season of living and enjoying what it means to be young, and for the first time they got to do it without the inevitable heartbreak of goodbyes looming as they always had before. There were boys that broke both their hearts at different times, but as each girl recovered from the embarrassment of her heartbreak, she grew stronger in realizing that there was so much more to the world than their immature counterparts. They weren't confident, independent women by any means, but they were right where they needed to be and for once, they were exactly what they needed to be, and that was just two fifteen-year-old girls who were miles away from having everything figured out.

Across the country in a small town in Georgia, one family wished for nothing more than the love of their lives to have the same luxury. Jessica Morris had turned fourteen in February.

She'd been gone since December and although her family prayed without ceasing that she would be with them again, they were told to accept that the worst possibility had become true. But they refused.

When the search parties slowed, the Morris' created their own. When those waned, they spent every single day driving to neighboring towns and passing out fliers that had her picture and information on them. They saved every penny they had to offer a reward of $10,000 for her safe return. Yet no one knew anything and the calls with tips on her whereabouts seemed they would never come. But still they persisted.

And one day, a week before Mother's Day, Jessica's mother Janice received a text message. "This is getting boring. If you can find her, you can have her. Bring the $10,000, I need play money." In a message that followed was a picture of a meadow and two bare feet. She jammed the detective's number into her phone immediately and within minutes the full forces of their county, state, and federal law enforcement were in tow. No one knew what they were about to uncover, but it was the only tip that had arrived in the life of the investigation thus far that brought them so close, and they weren't about to dismiss it.

Janice Morris was fearless and so fiercely hopeful that she ran out of the police cruiser the second it halted.

They had screeched to a stop in a grassy opening that they were able to identify by zooming in on the picture that had been sent by the perpetrator. Since there was a public restroom in the distance behind it and there were only three in the area that were blue and only one on the edge of a meadow, the detectives knew exactly where to go.

She ran into the center of the clearing and screamed for her daughter as loud and clearly as she could. "JESSICA! Jess baby, I'm here. We're here, where are you?!" As she shouted, the police canvased the area all around her and it took only seconds before her daughter that she'd missed so terribly for every second of five months, two weeks, and three days was found. A note was affixed to the tree she'd been leaning against, blindfolded and almost dead. It gave specific instructions on where to leave the money, how, and when.

The family let the professionals deal with the specifics, but discovered later that eventually, the note would lead them to the same suspect they had their eye on all along. But their Jessica was alive, barely-but she wasn't gone and that was enough for them to keep holding on. It took weeks to rehydrate and nourish her to a point of sure survival. In fact, it was uncertain if she would make it even then, but like her parents and two siblings that had fought endlessly for her return, Jessica was a survivor.

She fought hard to get better and when she was able, she shared everything that she remembered.

Between her testimony and the handwriting from the note, the criminal analysis team was able to pinpoint that Aaron was not only the perpetrator, but that he had acted alone. His voice, the smells, the things he said to her, and most importantly, the evidence they'd found on Jessica's body completed the circle of evidence needed to arrest him for her kidnapping, torture, and aggravated assault.

It was only a matter of a search warrant and his lawyer's failure to deliver the usual loophole bypassing that landed him in court yet again. Aaron had been suspected early in the trial because he'd been seen giving her a ride home from school the day before she disappeared. He had raped her for the first time that day and she told her parents. Aaron had said if she told anyone that he'd kill her, but she had been raised right and knew that no matter what, she told if someone hurt her.

So, she did, but all she could say was that he was a stranger. She hadn't known him, but she knew the color of his car, and that his skin was olive and he was handsome. It wasn't enough to catch him at first, but her parents had immediately called the police and filed a report anyway.

Jessica wouldn't go to the hospital for a sexual assault kit because she was absolutely mortified and all she could see in her mind was his face. All she could hear was the promise of him coming back and hurting her worse. So, she stayed home, and went to bed, knowing only that a handsome boy in a nice red car was the devil himself and she never wanted to see him again. And to make her biggest fear and worst nightmare come true, he returned in the night and kidnapped her from her room while her family slept.

    The following morning, Janice went in to check on her daughter. It was only 4am and her bed was empty, the window open. She screamed for her husband and again, dialed the police. The response was immediate, and an APB went out for a young man in a red sports car. They whittled it down to five in town, and eventually got a lead that suggested that Aaron could be a suspect. Along with the time of day and the neighborhood she was taken from, they had enough to bring him in. The pieces began to fall together, and his name and face were plastered all over TV. And like money has a way of doing, blind eyes were suddenly being turned by people that mattered, and what felt like a certainty became a convenient mystery. But in the end, DNA couldn't lie. Money couldn't bury the evil, and Aaron was tried as an adult and went to jail to serve a twenty-year sentence.

Willow chose to press charges for her assault as well. She waited until the Jessica Morris trial was over so that it didn't get pushed under the table, and just prayed that it wouldn't become a public circus. She didn't want to see him in person, and she most definitely didn't want to have to do so with the entire world watching, and luckily, she didn't have to. Because of the time that had passed, there was no physical evidence to test and there were no witnesses to what had happened. Aaron of course denied ever having met her, but for the second time, DNA couldn't lie, and Elijah's paternity test was confirmed.

So, Willow persisted, and because of the threat of increased defamation of the family name, his father, the Senator of Georgia, settled with them out of court in a settlement so large she almost couldn't believe it. She didn't want the money, she wanted justice and there was no way she would get it. But she did the best she could with the situation-she used the settlement to set up a fund for Elijah's future so that he would never want for anything. With the understanding that he would never know where the money came from, she handed the trust over to her parents and prayed that her son would choose wisely for his life when he was old enough to. Whatever he did, all she wanted for him was happiness. She knew money couldn't buy that for him, but it could make the road there a little bit easier.

She did reserve five percent of the settlement to help support the local teen pregnancy center as well; she hoped that any girl unlucky enough to end up in her position would have the resources she needed to make as informed of a decision as Willow got to, and with as much support as she was given.

♥

Elijah was fourteen when Willow gave him a special birthday present. He'd been begging for a new bike so he could go to the skatepark and ride in the bowl and on the ramps. He was active and full of energy and life. Unlike her, Elijah was tall. His arms and legs were lanky, and he had an easy muscle tone that persisted with almost no physical exertion. He had permanently tan skin and his mother's blue eyes. He was kind, funny, and full of random facts that he shared with anyone that would listen. There wasn't a cell of musical talent in his body, but he lived for capturing the world through pictures. Academia was neither easy or difficult for him, and he did what he had to so he could get through school. But his laugh, it was just exactly like his Dad Max's.

Willow had become a woman that resembled both of her own parents. She had her mom's curvy and short stature and her dad's dark curly hair and ice blue eyes. Her style wasn't anything like either of them, with her tendency toward cowboy boots, bootcut jeans, and comfortable old t-shirts from bands they'd seen on tour over the years. It was a far cry from the alternative teenager she had once been, but Willow was very much her own woman without a concern about who she may or may not be impressing with her looks. That said, it was a rare day that Willow was seen by others (strangers or familiar) that didn't appreciate just how naturally beautiful she was.

Her wit had been sharpened by an unwillingness to rocket into adulthood after her son's birth. Instead, she used her life experience to color her humor and fuel her desire to live along a timeline that was slower than her peers. As a result, she was considered a late bloomer when it came to seriously dating, the clown of her class, and the person everyone wanted to be around because what she exuded was joy.

It seemed to be a novel take on growing older when her peers were in a hurry to experience the kind of things that Willow had already endured. She knew the truth about making choices older than a kid is prepared to handle. She still had stretch marks to remind her what a handsome stranger's smile could lead to, and nightmares of what nearly became her fate at the hand of the same sick person. But as she looked at Elijah, there wasn't a day she regretted his existence. It was her proudest feat to have given him life, and the love that poured from her family into him as he grew was all she could have ever asked for. Her beginnings hadn't been normal, and her choices had brought her there, so she dedicated the rest of her life to slowing down and enjoying the view as she started over at the age of fifteen.

When she had arrived at the house, she stepped down out of her tall '78 F-150.

She had a small hobby farm of her own in the neighboring town of Boris and she was a large animal vet there. Sunday dinner was a constant in her family; they'd done it for as long as she could remember, and this night was fittingly a Sunday as well.

She texted Jarod, her boyfriend of three years, to let him know she'd gotten there safely. A good man of strong character, he was working swing shift but had sent a video message wishing Elijah a happy birthday. He told the kid to get ready because it was on next week when he had the day off, and he was going to whoop him in the racing game this time. As she closed the message, Willow smiled and thought to herself, *I really should marry that man. He's going to stop asking me if I keep putting him off.* At this, she chuckled a little, knowing full well that Jarod would be the man she'd spend the rest of her life with. She just liked to see him squirm a little, so she refused to accept his proposals which came often and were more extravagant each time. Before he hired a sky writer, she figured she should take him up on his offer. Worst yet, he may give up one day, and that wouldn't be cute or funny at all. *Yep, it's probably time to jump*, she thought.

As she shoved her phone into her back pocket, her dark curls caught in the wind as she looked over her parents' property. She loved everything about it there.

Her door creaked as she opened it wide and pulled out the gift she'd brought Elijah. Her heart jumped a little as she looked at it one last time and refused to let the scenario of him freaking out and yelling at her or storming off replay in her mind again. It had haunted her enough times already, and it was too late to turn back now. This was the moment; she knew it in the depths of her soul. It just happened to be one of the rare ones that could lay tread on the path of her relationship with the kid, for the rest of their lives. *No big deal, Will, it's gonna be fine. He will be fine. Stop being a wackadoo, we got this...* Her mind was busy trying to convince her to stop worrying when she was greeted by her uncle J, who had all but catapulted out the front door to come greet her with a high five and a high-pitched giggle.

    She smiled and her brain sighed with relief as she greeted one of her favorite people in the world. "J! I missed you!" She slapped her palm against his in the air and twirled around and bumped her right hip against his in their usual ritual. "Whoa, missed you!" He replied with a huge smile. "Lij birthday! Cake, Whoa! PIZZA!" As had always been true, J couldn't conceal his joy-especially when it came to pizza. It wasn't a Friday when he usually ate it and that seemed to build on his excitement.

He escorted her to the house, opened the front door for her (as her dad had taught him to for a lady), and she stepped into the house where everything that was important had ever happened to her. Willow was home.

She greeted her parents with big hugs and motioned Elijah over to do the same. He rolled his eyes in pretend annoyance. She returned his teenage behavior with a noogie to mess up his perfectly placed hair and a playful smile that dared him to return it. And he did, making a rat's nest out of her bouncing curls which resulted in a wrestling match that ended in Willow bear hugging the young teen who was easily four inches taller than her already.

"Happy birthday Lij," she told him with her electric smile as she handed him the box she'd wrapped in bright green wrapping paper. She'd never tell anyone she had wrapped and rewrapped it six times with different paper, afraid that she wouldn't be able to dress the gift just right. And it needed to be. But in the end, she'd settled on his favorite color, and it felt perfect.

As he picked up the box that was far too small to include a bike, he pretended to be excited. His eyebrows raised and his voiced cracked as he thanked his sister for the gift. "Hey, thanks Will..." he smiled and tried to be convincing. Before she could respond, J started jumping up and down and wiggling.

He screeched a shrill high-pitched scream, "Ohhhhh! Open it! Yay!" Ror's eyes flashed at Max who was already preparing to do some slow breathing with J as he stifled a laugh and said, "Alright J, let's calm it down. He's opening it." J let out one more little whoop and begin controlling his breaths. Willow accepted her mother's arms around her shoulders in a tight squeeze as she stood above her daughter, and they waited anxiously.

    Elijah wondered what all the excitement could be about and ripped open the lime green paper and lifted off the lid to the box. Inside it was a notebook with Spiderman on the front. He looked at Willow curiously and she smiled back at him, her crystal blue eyes sparkling. Max and Ror made an excuse to leave the room, inviting Jordan to help them get cake and ice cream ready, which was met with a loping hightail to the kitchen. Willow sat down and patted the couch next to her and told Elijah, "Get over here kid, I want to read the first entry with you. It's been a while since I've seen this thing!" He grabbed the faded notebook, opened the front cover, and hesitantly began to read. As he took in the words on the page in front of him, he turned his head and studied Willow, beginning to realize the implication of what he read.

He frowned and stared, realizing for the first time that it was like looking into his own eyes that were wide and kind and had lashes that were so thick they looked layered. Elijah's head tilted, a silent question in his movement. Willow nodded back at him, and he asked the question he didn't quite understand yet. "So, what, you're actually my, my...Mom?" She looked back at her son and for the first time in his life, she was able to admit, "Yeah Lij, I am. Or at least your mother. I'm sorry if it's the weirdest, dude. Trust me, I know. There's a lot more you're about to find out in there, and some of it's going to be crazy. Especially at the end. Just know that I gave you this because you can handle it, and because you deserve to know. And... I just really, really love you Lij."

His body was limp with confusion, but Elijah hugged the woman that had been raised to be his sister. He wasn't sure what to think, but he read on. Just as he was taking in the intense and emotional words that described the day of his birth, Elijah was interrupted when the lights cut to black. As he looked up, he was welcomed with the flicker of fourteen candles swaying gently in the dark and his parents and J as they walked into the room with his cake.

"Happy birthday to you... Happy birthday to you! Happy birthday dear Elijah..." The words he'd heard every year before that day suddenly felt extra special.

As his family surrounded him with smiles, his mom set the cake on the table in front of him. Elijah blew out the candles, made a wish, and knew that his life would never be the same again. But as he looked over at Willow and back at his parents and J, he realized that no matter how weird or screwed up their reality might be, he was just lucky to have them all. The rest would sort itself out, and he hoped he'd understand it all better when he was done reading the mysterious notebook Willow gave him. But for now, he was ready to have some sprinkle cake and chocolate ice cream and find out where Dad had hidden the bike that he was positive was waiting somewhere in the house.

Before Elijah could consider where it could be stashed, Max began the countdown. "Alright kid, you know it's here. You've got three minutes to find your bike or you have to wait 'til tomorrow to ride it!" And with that, the search was on. Elijah raced around the house, thinking about what a local legend he was about to become at the skatepark in his hometown of Avery, Oregon. As she watched with the childish glee that pushed him on, Willow smiled and was so grateful that her son was every bit of the immature, lively, and naïve fourteen-year-old that he deserved to be.

# About the author

Danielle is a native Oregonian that has been writing most of her life. Willow Dawn is her second book, a sequel to her debut novel Jordan Blue which was re-released in 2021. She enjoys being in the mountains and spending time with the people that give her life color and meaning. Professionally, Danielle has spent over fifteen years in the field of human services.

CPSIA information can be obtained
at www.ICGtesting.com
Printed in the USA
LVHW031547200522
719343LV00006B/467